A HUSBAND FOR VICTORIA

CYNTHIA WOOLF

Firehouse Publishing

Published by Firehouse Publishing
Woolf, Cynthia

For Jim, my best friend, my husband and my love.

CHAPTER ONE

November 17, 1870—New York City

Just outside the library of the great house where she worked, Victoria Coleman stood trying to stop the dizziness that had plagued her for the last few days. She'd even fainted twice but luckily she was in her bedroom so no one knew. Now she was in the hall next to the door to the library, her arm braced on the wall and breathed deeply.

Her knees gave way.

When she opened her eyes, she saw the Mosaic ceiling in the library.

"Victoria." Mr. Thomas, his kind brown eyes filled with worry, knelt next to her and patted her cheek. "Victoria, are you all right?"

"Wh...what? Oh!" She sat up quickly and immediately wished she hadn't, falling back to the rich green brocade of the couch. "I'm so sorry, Mr. Thomas. You must think me the worst ninny for fainting."

"Not at all. I think something must be terribly wrong. Tell

me, so I can help. Has my wife been working you too hard?" His brown hair was sprinkled with gray, even though he was just thirty-five-years old. Probably from being married to Mildred. She was a horrible person and in some ways frightened Victoria.

Victoria shook her head and began to cry. "I'm...I'm with child, sir. I...I was violated several months ago by my friend Adele's husband. She left to get something from the grocer and he attacked me. I haven't been back and I know she wonders why, but I won't hurt her by telling her. Nothing can be done about it and the knowledge will only make her life miserable, as she can't leave him. She has no place to go. I didn't want to tell anyone because I was afraid I'd be sacked and I have nowhere to go either."

He patted her hand, and then released her, letting her hand fall back to the rich green brocade of the sofa. He sat next to her on the sofa. "You're safe here for as long as you want. Are you all right now?"

"Yes, thank you for your kindness."

He frowned. "I can't very well throw you out into the street. What kind of man would that make me?"

"A typical man." She slapped a hand over her mouth. "I'm sorry. That was terrible of me when you've been so nice."

Mr. Thomas chuckled. "Given what you've seen of men, I don't wonder at your opinion of us."

Victoria released a breath and gave him a small smile, still unsure of what he might want for his kindness.

He stepped away and put his arms behind his back. "Well, if you're feeling better, I'm sure Margie is missing her favorite person."

She shook her head. "Oh, no, sir. I'm sure you are her favorite person."

He laughed. "Not my wife, huh?"

"Oh, no, sir." She slapped her hand over her mouth again. "I'm sorry. I meant nothing untoward about your wife."

He waved his hand in front of her. "No offense taken. I know what a shrew I married. Maybe that's why I find your niceness so refreshing."

She dipped her head and her cheeks heated. "Thank you, sir. You are too kind, but I must return to Margie. She'll come looking for me and only get in trouble for being out of the nursery."

He held out his hand.

She took it, and he helped her to her feet.

"I suggest next time, you sit first."

Bowing her head, she said, "Yes, sir, I will."

She hurried out of the library, past Mrs. Thomas, who lifted an eyebrow and sneered. Though she looked just like Margie, with her blonde hair and blue eyes. She may have been beautiful on the outside, but she was ugly inside.

Victoria had passed the foyer and was just about to start up the wide staircase when she heard the library door slam. Even with the door shut she heard Mrs. Thomas's screechy voice yell at her husband.

"You've gotten that girl pregnant, haven't you?"

Mr. Thomas held his own and hollered back.

"You don't know what you're talking about, Mildred."

Victoria realized they were arguing about her. Not wanting to hear anymore, she lifted her skirt and walked up the stairs to the nursery. She was slower than normal, her legs still a little weak.

———

Victoria found Margie right where she'd left her. The little blonde, blue-eyed girl was having tea with her dollies and a stuffed bear.

Victoria sat on one of the small wooden chairs. She remembered the first time she'd sat on one after she'd seen Mr. Thomas sitting on one having tea with Margie. She'd laughed at the sight, but knew the chair would hold her if it held him.

He'd looked up and smiled. "Victoria would you like to join us for tea? One seat is available. Mr. Bear has the other."

She placed fingers over her mouth to hide her smile and nodded. If he could do it, so could she.

Today she gazed around the nursery knowing she'd have to leave soon. They wouldn't let her stay and have her baby here. So, looking around, she saw all she would miss. The nursery was a huge room. Margie's bed was there. On one end of the room, along with the little table, and a toy box, was a bookshelf for books and her dolls. A desk and blackboard were on the other end with her bed in the middle.

The room was painted a pale, robin's egg blue, and the heavy, dark blue curtains had stars and moons on them. Her bed had a spread that matched the curtains.

Victoria loved this room, and she loved Margie. Victoria had been with the Thomases since Margie was born and had raised her for the last three years. Though she hated to say goodbye, Victoria knew she'd have to.

For now, though, she'd have tea with her favorite little girl and not think about what tomorrow might bring.

————

The next morning, Mrs. Thomas burst into the kitchen where Victoria and Margie were eating their breakfast.

"Ah, Victoria, I knew I could find you lollygagging with my daughter."

Victoria stood. At five feet eight she was about four inches taller than Mrs. Thomas and the woman now had to look up to her. "We are not lollygagging, madam. We are having breakfast and I'll be glad to do whatever you need me to after the meal is complete."

"Yes, whatever." She waved her arm dismissively. When you're done, you will escort Margery to the nursery and then you will report to the kitchen. I fired the scullery maid, and you'll now be doing her chores."

Even though she was shocked at this turn of events, Victoria kept her voice neutral. "Madam, how am I to take care of Margie if I'm here in the kitchen?"

"I'll handle Margery until I can get in another governess to care for her."

"You're making me a scullery maid permanently?" Victoria's voice rose to a high pitch. The work was harder and might not be good for her baby, but then that is probably what Mrs. Thomas is hoping for.

Mrs. Thomas smiled.

It was the evilest smile Victoria had ever seen.

"Yes. If you wish to work here, that is your new position."

Needing the job, Victoria frowned but answered, "Yes, ma'am."

She escorted Margie to the nursery.

When Victoria tried to leave, the child cried and was distraught.

"I must go, sweetheart. Your mama has given me orders to change my position here and I have no choice. I'll see you when you come for meals. Don't worry."

"No. I don't want you to go," she said between sniffles.

"I have to." She hugged the little girl. "Now you go play with your dollies. Your mama or Daddy will be up soon."

Mr. Thomas walked into the nursery. "Sooner than you expected. Victoria may I see you in the hall, please?"

"Certainly." She led the way out.

He shut the door behind them. "I've talked to my wife

and made clear that you are the governess for as long as you're here, but Victoria, she will get worse. She thinks your baby is mine and wants you to lose it. Mildred doesn't want anyone to interfere with Margery's inheritance. You really must leave to be safe. I don't trust her as far as you are concerned." He handed her one-hundred and fifty dollars. "This will give you a decent start. You'll need new clothes as you increase and a new pair of boots as well. Try to get what you need here. I've heard the prices out West are atrocious. But you must leave as soon as possible. I've written an introduction letter to Mrs. Emily Johnson, owner of Brides for the West. She runs a boarding house and also matches her ladies to men in the West who need wives. I believe you should do this."

She shook her head. *I can't go into the wild. What do I know of shooting animals and cooking over a fire or living in a tent? I've seen those dime novels about Jim Bridger and Kit Carson.* "Out West? In the wild? A bride to some strange man? I don't think I could."

"You will if you want this baby to have a good chance to survive. You can't make a living as a governess with a child of your own. You know that as well as I do. Most families want a governess who will devote herself totally to the family, not to her own child. If I could I'd hire you at one of the banks I own, but you know that women do not work in banks." He took her by the shoulders. "Do this for the baby and for you. Please."

She pulled away from him, but realized he was right, and she wanted what was best for her baby. Taking a deep breath, she nodded. "Very well, I'll leave tonight after everyone is in bed."

"Good. I like you and don't want to see you come to harm. I believe that Mildred is capable of harming you."

Victoria wrung her hands. Her heart beat a rapid tattoo as

fear gripped her. "After seeing her this morning, I believe she is *planning* on hurting me. I knew from hearing your argument that she believes the baby is yours, but I thought she would want it not try to kill it. Perhaps you should worry about Margie."

He shook his head. "Margie isn't in danger. Mildred doesn't want anyone to share Margie's inheritance. But I don't know how far her greed will take her. I never should have married her, but I had no choice, she seduced me you see and became pregnant, or so I thought."

"Forgive me for speaking so boldly but are you sure you're the only man she seduced? Margie doesn't look like you, but then you know that." She gazed up at him and realized the truth. "You know she's not your child, yet you love her just the same."

He shrugged. "I knew as soon as Margie was born that she wasn't my child. She was born two months too early, but the minute I held her, she was mine. I love her more than life itself."

"You're a good father. I hope that someday you find a woman who truly loves you and will give you children of your own." She lifted herself on tiptoe and kissed his cheek.

"I knew I'd find you two together." Mildred's scratchy voice came from the top of the stairs. "I'll make you both pay. You just wait and see." She turned and ran down the stairs.

Victoria turned toward the stairs.

Mr. Thomas did the same.

He turned to Victoria. "I don't think you can wait until tonight. I want you to pack your things and leave now. I'll stay with you and see you out the front door then I'll come back here for Margie. I believe Mildred has become quite unhinged."

Victoria's heart pounded and her hands were sweaty. She

was sure Mildred would kill her. Victoria hurried to her bedroom next to Margie's.

He followed her but waited at the door rather than follow her in.

"You may enter, Mr. Thomas."

"No, thank you. I can watch for Mildred out here."

Victoria nodded and hurried to put only her necessary clothes into a large carpetbag. The rest would stay, probably to be shredded by Mrs. Thomas, but Victoria needed to travel light. She didn't know how far she was traveling.

"Here let me take that for you. You'll have long enough to carry it."

"Did you see Mrs. Thomas?"

He shook his head as he took the carpetbags from her. "No. That's what worries me."

"Shall we go anyway? Is it safe?"

"She won't hurt you with me along. And when I don't go with you, she'll think she's won, so hopefully that will be the end of it. Do you have the letter to Mrs. Johnson? She's a dear friend. Her husband and I were college friends and when he married Emily, she became a great friend, too. Unfortunately, her husband died in debt, so I did what I could and helped her set up this business. She's made quite a go of it in the last few years."

She held up her reticule. "In here, along with twenty dollars of the money. The rest is in my boot."

He furrowed his brows.

"I put it there while packing my clothes."

"Oh, and here I thought you were just changing your shoes."

She shrugged. "Well, I did that, too. I wasn't sure how far I must walk."

"Not too far. You can take a trolley almost to her front door."

"That's good, for me anyway. I won't have long to walk."

When they reached the door, Victoria turned. "Thank you. You've been very good to me and I appreciate it."

His smile was sad. "Margie and I will miss you very much. The only reason living with Mildred was tolerable was because of you. Seeing your smiling face every morning was enough to last the day. I'm just sorry I can't do more for you."

She rose to her tiptoes and kissed his cheek. "Perhaps we'll see each other again."

"I will hold out that hope. Now go before she comes down the hall."

Victoria nodded and headed down the driveway to the trolley two blocks away. She was actually glad she wasn't leaving in the middle of the night. She wasn't sure she could. Since the rape, even though it had been in her friend's home, she didn't like being out in the dark. But now at mid-morning she felt safe and hurried to the station.

She arrived at Brides for the West about an hour after leaving the Thomases' home. The door was a bright green and stood out amidst the brown doors of the surrounding buildings.

After knocking, she turned the knob and walked inside. The room was fairly small. Three folded legal document files stood behind an oak desk and a potbelly stove stood in the corner. The room was painted a pale green that Victoria found soothing.

Seated behind the desk was a blonde woman in her early forties. As Victoria entered the woman looked up then stood. "Welcome, my dear. Come in."

Victoria walked over and sat in the Windsor style wooden chair, this one with just four dowels, making it look like the window of a jail cell. She put her carpet bag on the floor in front of her.

"What can I do for you, dear?"

"Mr. David Thomas wrote you this letter." She pulled the letter from her reticule and handed the woman the envelope.

Mrs. Johnson opened the envelope and read the missive. When finished, she turned her attention to Victoria and smiled gently. "Well, my dear, David says you've found yourself in quite a pickle. I'm sure I can help you. He also said to send him the bill for you to live at the boarding house for as long as necessary."

Victoria's eyes filled with tears. "He's so kind. I don't know how I'll ever repay him."

"He's a good man and a good friend. He would never expect you to repay his kindness, which is his way of doing things."

"Yes, he's a good man."

"That's why he puts up with Mildred, so he can be with Margie."

Victoria played with the strings of her reticule. "I understand. Do you think you can find a husband for me, Mrs. Johnson?"

"Oh, I'm sure I can and please, call me Emily. We will live together for a while. Now, tell me about yourself. I take it you have no family to depend upon for help."

"That's correct. I was raised in an orphanage. The sisters, while kind, were strict disciplinarians. They would have thrown me out into the street upon learning of my pregnancy, regardless of how it happened. I look forward to raising this child with love instead of just tending to its basic needs."

Emily folded her hands on top of the desk. "How did it happen? David didn't say."

Victoria stared down at her lap. "My best friend's husband violated me. I couldn't tell her but have not been back to see her since it happened so she must have figured out something is wrong. I don't know. She hasn't contacted me nor I her in three months."

"How long do you think you can hide the pregnancy?"

"I don't know. I need a larger corset now. I've got this one extended as far as it will go."

"Very well. We'll go on a shopping trip tomorrow. For the man I have in mind, you'll need a thick, woolen coat and heavy boots and shoes. He's a rancher in the Colorado Territory and I understand the winters there can be freezing. And you'll be slogging around in mud and muck. Some of my previous brides have said that they have had to milk cows, gather eggs and feed the chickens. I'm afraid you won't be a governess any longer. You'll be expected to cook, clean, and anything else expected of a rancher's wife, which might be any or all of the things I mentioned."

It will be like being back at the orphanage—milk the cows, feed the chickens, gather the eggs, slop the hogs. "I realize that I'll be starting a new life. As long as I have a good place to raise my child, I'll do whatever I have to."

Emily clapped her hands and stood. "Let's go get you settled in the boarding house." She came around the desk and put her arm through the crook in Victoria's elbow. "Then we'll talk about who is available to marry you. And I think you should be a widow and explain your pregnancy that way. You'll be Mrs. Victoria Coleman. I don't normally advocate lying to your prospective groom but I don't see how you have any choice in the matter. "

"That would make it easier for everyone I believe."

Emily nodded and, once outside, she linked her arm with Victoria's as they walked next door. "I agree. And as far as your friendship with your friend, it is over whichever way you choose. This way you'll be safe and so will your baby."

Going up the seven steps to a stoop, she entered the parlor. In the back of the room on the right was the staircase. A hall with rooms on either side led to the back of the house.

Emily pointed at the stairs. "The bedrooms are all upstairs

except mine, which is down this hall. At the end is the kitchen."

She followed Emily single file down the hall. Both the parlor and the hall were covered in wallpaper with roses on vines. It was quite lovely.

"To my left is my bedroom. Across the hall is my office and library. As long as the door is open you may enter anytime. If it is closed, it means I'm working and you must knock, though I prefer not to be disturbed unless it's an emergency."

Victoria thought she would only be there one night. "Do I really need all this information?"

"Perhaps not, but you could be here for more than one night if we can't get you on the train right away. You must change trains, too. Having only two carpetbags, as you will after our shopping trip, will make the travel much easier."

Victoria nodded. "Yes, I suppose so." She'd never been on a train and travelled two hundred miles much less across the country.

Entering the kitchen, its size surprised her, but with a kitchen table that sat twelve the room had to be big. A four-burner stove stood to her right, with a butler's pantry *and* a regular pantry next to the stove. Along the back wall were cupboards above the counter and drawers and more cupboards below, along with the sink and icebox. The window over the sink overlooked a small courtyard.

"Every part of the house I've seen so far has been lovely."

"Thank you. I try to keep it nice for the girls. Let's sit, shall we? I can make tea or a pot of coffee on the stove. Which do you prefer?"

"I'd like the coffee. I need to get used to it. I would imagine they prefer it on the ranch. Mr. Thomas always preferred coffee."

Emily poured coffee for both of them. "I like the coffee

first thing in the morning but prefer tea as the day wears on and in the evening.

"I'll send food with you for the first day, but you will need to buy food along the way. I understand the box lunches made and sold by the local housewives are the way to go. They are cheaper and much tastier than the restaurant food."

"Mr. Thomas gave me money to cover all my expenses and give me a new start in a new land. Now I best go shopping for those clothes you said I need and a second carpetbag."

"Wonderful. David is a good man and a good friend. He helped me get on my feet when my husband died and I found myself in dire straits. Let me get, Jane, my assistant to watch the office and I'll go with you. I need the time off, anyway."

Victoria grinned. "Oh, good, I hate shopping by myself. I used to go with Adele, but that hasn't been possible, for obvious reasons."

Emily tilted her head to the right and stood. "You know, so do I. Maybe I'll do a little shopping, too. But first I'll show you to a room. Dinner is at six and I would suggest you have a bath tonight. You won't get another one for at least nine, probably ten days. Even if I hear from your proposed husband tomorrow you won't be able to leave until the next day."

Victoria set her coffee cup on the table and stood. After picking up her carpetbag, she followed Emily. "Thank you for being so kind to me. I know that even with the letter from Mr. Thomas, you didn't need to be."

"You're welcome. You've had a bad time of it and seemed to need a friend."

No one *will ever treat me like that again*. Ever. *I'd rather die than endure another assault.*

CHAPTER TWO

Sunday, December 4, 1871

Victoria was doing the breakfast dishes at the boarding house. They still hadn't had a response to Emily's wire.

"Victoria. Victoria." Emily came in waving a piece of paper in her hand. "I've finally gotten a response to my wire to Mr. Andrew Mayfield. He is the rancher I told you about. He would love to have you for a wife and wishes for you to come to Golden City immediately."

Victoria turned, wiped her soapy hands on a dish towel and then set it aside. She leaned back against the double porcelain sink. "Really? He's willing to take on a pregnant wife?"

"Well..."

Emily's shoulders slumped and she lowered her chin.

"You didn't tell him, did you?"

She looked away from Victoria. "He said he would accept any woman, with or without children, and you will be a woman with a child. Just not right away."

Victoria wrung her hands, turned and began to pace in front of the counters and the sink. "I need to get away from here. If I stick around Mildred is liable to find me."

Emily let out a deep breath. "There is always that possibility, I won't deny it. Mildred knows what I do, that I help young women find husbands. It won't take her long to come knocking on my door."

Victoria turned to Emily. "If I'm gone and she comes here, she wouldn't have any reason to think I was ever here."

"That's true and I won't mention you at all."

"Thank you. May we have a cup of tea and you can tell me all about the rancher I'm supposed to marry?" She went to the table and sat.

While Emily prepared the tea, she talked about the man she had for Victoria. "His name is Andrew Mayfield. He has a two-year-old daughter. Six months ago, he lost his wife and son in childbirth—"

"What!" Victoria widened her eyes and practically flew to her feet. "Six months ago! You don't think it's a little too soon to have a pregnant woman in his home again?"

"No, now come to the office with me and listen."

Victoria picked up her teacup and followed Emily to the office.

Emily sat behind the desk.

Victoria sat in front of it.

"I normally wouldn't suggest this but if you don't tell him right away, I believe it will be fine. Look at you," she waved her hand up and down in front of Victoria. "You don't show yet and won't for a while. By that time you will have him in love with you and he'll accept your pregnancy and then your child as well."

"I don't know. I don't feel right. I'll have to undress and dress in the dark for him not to notice."

"Well, if you want to tell him before you marry you can,

but I believe this man is the best match for you. Look, Victoria, you could be the best thing to happen to him. Being there could help him heal from his wife's death."

"Or he could hate me and throw me and the baby out into the street."

She came to the front of the desk and leaned against it. "He won't do that. Trust me. He needs you. Remind him he needs someone to care for Susannah. She's his little girl."

Victoria placed her teacup on the desk. "Well, I'm ready to go. I believe you and I must find a husband and a home. The farther away from New York, the better."

"I'll wire him tomorrow, and we can get you on the train to Denver. You must take the stagecoach to Golden City." Emily set her teacup on the desk and took a paper from one of the drawers. She ran her finger part-way down the page and then looked up with a smile. "If you leave tomorrow, which is the fifth, you should arrive in Golden City on, Saturday, December tenth. It takes about six days to Denver and then another two to three hours by stage to Golden City, depending on your driver. Mr. Mayfield sent money for standard passage."

Victoria swallowed hard. *Six days on a train. How will I stay clean? I will not waste my money on premium accommodations.* "I've never traveled by train before. Have any tips or suggestions of what I should do to make my trip more pleasant?"

"Carry a washcloth and towel with you. You'll need them to keep clean and refresh yourself periodically. Keep your overcoat on at all times if the windows are open. Ash and dirt come in and will cover your coat, but at least your clothes will remain unsoiled."

"What about my hair?"

"I'd tell you to wear a cloth on your head, but that isn't practical. You must hope your hat protects you from the worst of the dirt."

"This all sounds good, and to be honest, rather intimidating, but I'm ready."

———

Victoria had never been outside New York City. Never seen the small towns and farms that she passed on the way to Chicago.

From Chicago to Denver, she saw lots of animals out in the open spaces. From her reading of the dime novels she picked up, she knew that the lithe, jumping animal with horns was an antelope. The huge, furry animal was called a buffalo. There were hundreds, maybe even thousands that crossed the tracks in front and behind the train. So many times the train had to stop while the animals moved around the train and over the tracks. The land was brown with mud and yellow grass, the snow out of sight.

After arriving in Denver, she boarded a stagecoach bound for Golden. This in itself was another adventure. Luckily, Victoria got a seat by the window. She could look out at the landscape they crossed but more importantly she had fresh air.

She checked the watch on her wrist and saw that it was about nine-thirty in the morning. The coach should reach Golden City before lunch. She hoped he would let them get lunch before the drive to his ranch. She was starving.

Inside the coach was stifling. The unwashed bodies of the passengers almost made her nauseous even though she realized she probably smelled little better.

———

December 10, 1870

. . .

Six days after leaving New York, Victoria arrived in Golden late in the afternoon, exhausted. Sitting up for those six days on the train and then the bone-jarring two-hour ride in the stagecoach had her feeling like an old rag doll that had been beat to death.

The stagecoach driver helped her down from the coach and handed her the two carpetbags that held everything she owned.

"Thank you, Mr. Jones."

He tipped his hat. "You're welcome, Mrs. Coleman. You take care."

"Thank you, I will."

She looked around and walked up the steps to the board-walk in front of the Golden West Hotel. The location gave her a slightly higher vantage point from which to survey the surrounding town and look for Mr. Mayfield. Surveying the town up and down the street, she was too busy to pay atten-tion to those behind her.

The air was cold and her breath was visible. The buildings kept her from seeing much and to be honest, the scenery didn't interest her as much as finding her prospective husband.

"Mrs. Coleman?"

She screeched and jumped. "Good grief. You startled me, sir. Are you Mr. Andrew Mayfield?" She raised her gaze to the face of the tall man next to her. He was taller than her by a good six inches, even in her boots, and though she couldn't see his eyes, she saw his chiseled jaw and the firm set of his mouth. His lips were not too full and not too thin, though right now, they weren't very welcoming either.

"I am. Are these all your bags?" He picked up her two carpetbags.

"Yes. That's it."

"Follow me." He turned and started walking.

At the end of the boardwalk, in the alley next to the Golden City Mercantile, stood a wagon. As they got closer she saw that it was filled with large bags and boxes of canned goods and smaller bags. She looked up and saw the bench was just a plain wooden plank and stifled a groan. *Great, another ride on a board with no padding. Her poor bottom was already hurting.*

He helped her into the wagon before going around the back and climbing in next to her. Then he released the brake and slapped the reins on the animals' bottoms.

She did her best to stay on her side of the bench but it was narrow and her skirts rode against his leg. His very muscular leg. She'd noticed when he walked the way the muscles moved. The man definitely worked for a living.

"Are we going to your ranch now?"

He shook his head. "Not until we visit the preacher. He knows we're coming. I won't have my wife's reputation besmirched."

Oh God. He'll never accept me after he finds out I'm pregnant, but I'm not telling him, especially now. I need the protection of the marriage. Perhaps we can pass the baby off as his and just arriving early. Who was she kidding? As soon as the baby was born everyone would know she was expecting before they married. They would look at her with contempt and at Andrew with sympathy. This parallels the Thomases situation so much. I hope that doesn't mean we'll have the same kind of marriage. Will I become a shrew like Mildred?

Even if he loves me by then, will he look at the baby and always resent it because of the way it was conceived? I have to hope that Andrew is a good and honorable man, and like Mr. Thomas, that he will treat the child like his own.

"You said we're going to the preacher? Right now?"

"Yup. Can't take you to the ranch unless we're married."

Victoria swallowed hard. "But I thought we'd get to know each other a little before we got married."

"You've got about ten minutes." He slapped the reins on the horses bottoms. "I'll answer any question you have."

I have to know what to expect. Since the rape, I'm scared to have relations but he probably expects it. He is after all a man and will be a married man. I must do my duty. "Do you expect to have relations with me tonight?"

"Yes."

What if I can't develop a rapport with her like I did with Margie? What if she hates me? "Do you think your daughter will accept me as her mother?"

He shrugged. "It will probably take her some time, but she'll come around. She's only two."

His answers dismayed Victoria. "Who is watching her now?"

"My housekeeper, Mrs. Baldwin. You'll like her. She's a good woman, but she doesn't cook worth beans. I assume you cook." He slapped the reins again as the horses had slowed.

"I'm a passable cook, but I don't cook fancy. If that's what you want, you're marrying the wrong woman."

"The information on you said you are twenty-four. Is that correct?"

"Yes. And you are thirty-two, right?"

"I am."

She looked at his face and saw crinkle lines around his eyes which were the greenest green she'd ever seen. His hair was dark brown from what she could see under his hat and curled at the ends, just over his collar. She liked the way he looked.

It was hard to tell what the rest of him looked like as he was wearing a sheepskin coat buttoned up the front.

The wind blew, and she gathered her wool scarf over her ears.

He flipped up the collar of his coat.

In just a minute or two he pulled up at the house next to

the church. Then he set the brake before coming around to help her down.

"Thank you." A tingle passed from his hand to hers and she dropped her hand from his like it was a hot potato. She'd had no experience with men before Oliver's assault and the tingle surprised her.

He nodded and put his hand at her waist to guide her inside.

She felt like he needed to touch her for some reason.

Andrew knocked on the parsonage door.

A tall, austere woman answered.

She smiled at Andrew, and her face was totally transformed. She looked kind, friendly, even beautiful.

She likes Andrew. Was she friends with his wife? Will his friends accept me?

"Andrew. I wondered if we'd see you today. You said your bride was arriving." She turned toward Victoria. "That must be you. Victoria, if I'm not mistaken? We go little for convention out here. I'm Edna Bishop. My husband, Merle, is the reverend, though most of our congregation refers to him as the preacher." She smiled again.

"Thank you so much. I'm very glad to be here." Victoria was at ease, more so than she'd been since meeting Andrew Mayfield.

Edna took Victoria's hand and patted it. "Follow me." Edna led them to a small music room.

The reverend sat at the piano, looking somewhat frustrated. Suddenly he smashed his fingers onto the keys, in apparent frustration, before closing the top of the upright piano.

Edna's eyebrows lifted. "Merle, Andrew is here with his bride and I'm sure they are in a hurry. He'll want to get home to Susannah."

"Ah, Andrew." The reverend rose and came over with his right hand extended. "Good to see you, my boy."

Victoria smiled, despite her nerves, at the thought of anyone calling Andrew *boy*.

"We'll, get you two married and you'll be on your way." He turned to his wife. "Edna find Frances and we'll get this underway."

"I'm here, Daddy," said a young woman coming into the room. "Hello, Andrew." She came to Victoria. "And you must be Andrew's bride, Victoria. We've all be looking forward to meeting you."

The kindness of these people overcame Victoria. "Thank you."

She looked at Andrew and he was smiling. He didn't look as foreboding now as he did when they walked in.

"We'd like to get married now, Reverend. Can't be away from the ranch and Suse too long. She gets anxious when she knows I'm gone and it's not to work."

"Yes, yes. Let's get this started. You young people, stand in front of me, Andrew on my left."

They followed his instructions, and then Edna and Frances took their places.

"Good. Now, dearly beloved, we are gathered here in front of these witnesses and according to God's holy ordinance, to join this man and this woman in holy wedlock. Do you, Andrew John Mayfield, take this woman Victoria—" He arched his eyebrow.

"My middle name is June. Victoria June Coleman."

"Take this woman, Victoria June Coleman, as you're lawful wedded wife, to have and to hold, in sickness and in health, for richer or poorer, and to keep yourself only unto her for as long as you both shall live?"

"I do." Andrew's rich, deep baritone sounded loud and clear.

The reverend turned to her. "Do you, Victoria June Coleman, take this man, Andrew John Mayfield, to be your lawful wedded husband, to have and to hold, in sickness and in health, for richer or poorer, and to keep yourself only unto him for as long as you both shall live?"

Victoria looked at Andrew.

He smiled.

Though this was not the wedding she'd wanted as a girl, it was the best she could do and so necessary. Was she already breaking her wedding vows by not disclosing her pregnancy? Putting her thoughts and her fears aside, she answered. "I do." The clarity with which she answered surprised her.

"Then by the power vested in me by the Lord God Almighty and the Territory of Colorado, I now pronounce you man and wife. You may kiss the bride."

She turned to Andrew, expecting a quick kiss on the lips or the cheek.

He took her into his arms and kissed her, pressing his tongue into her mouth, tasting her, teasing her. She tasted the coffee he'd had she assumed with his breakfast.

She'd never been kissed before. After the surprise subsided, she returned his kiss as best she could. *Was this how all kisses between a man and his wife were? If so, she liked them very much.*

"Hmm. Hmm" The reverend cleared his throat.

Andrew relinquished her and smiled at the reverend. "Thanks, reverend." Then he handed the man a five-dollar gold piece. "For the church."

The man closed his fist around the gold piece. "So much money isn't necessary, Andrew, but the church thanks you for your kind donation."

Victoria knew that the reverend and his family lived on the kindness and donations from the congregation, at least the reverend at her church in New York had. The five dollars would buy them all a nice dinner and more if they decided to do that. She wasn't sure of the prices in town, but the ones she'd seen advertised on the windows of the Golden City Mercantile didn't seem much different from those in New York.

They walked outside. When she saw the wagon, Victoria couldn't help the groan that escaped.

Andrew stopped and turned to her. "What's the matter?"

"Nothing, really. It's just that I'm not looking forward to sitting on that hard seat again." She dropped her voice and looked around to make sure no one else could hear. "My nether regions are already sore from the stagecoach ride here from Denver."

"I should have thought of that. I have a folded-up blanket you can sit on. It will make the trip more comfortable."

When they got to the wagon, he reached under the seat and brought up the blanket, setting it on the bench. "There you go. That should help."

"Ah." She sighed after she sat. "Thank you. This is very kind. How long until we reach your ranch?"

"A little over two hours with the wagon, the horses can't pull it very fast. I live about twelve miles from town."

Once they were settled and on the way, Victoria's body relaxed. Many things still needed to be discussed, but not for a while. She would do her best to make him fall in love with her before she began to show and she figured she only had a month at most to do it.

CHAPTER THREE

Gorgeous blue sky framed majestic mountains, covered with trees and with snow on the peaks farther away. The scene was beautiful. On the left, was a flat mesa. In the valley between, where the small town lay were patches of snow broken up by spots of brown, dead grass and dirt. She thought...hoped...the land was prettier in the other seasons.

"Do you get all seasons of the year here?"

"Yes, why would you ask such a question?"

"Because some places I read about, it was practically summer all year 'round. I don't think I'd like that. I enjoy the differences between seasons."

"So do I."

At least we have that in common. "Tell me about your ranch."

"Well. I don't know how much I can tell you. It's a fair size, more than a thousand acres. I also have a string of about twenty horses, with more to come in the spring as several of the mares are expecting. Our dog, Daisy, will be having pups soon, too."

Victoria's hand went to her stomach before she realized and moved it back to her side.

"Are you hungry? I noticed you touch your stomach. Mrs. Baldwin made us a lunch. It's behind the seat, bring it up, and let's see what she packed."

Victoria lifted the heavy basket. She groaned and set it on the floorboards. "Oh, my. Did she pack for twelve people?"

He lifted his eyebrows. "No, just the two of us. Why?"

"Well, I see sandwiches, fried chicken, what looks like potato salad, cookies, a jar of tea. What would you like? I don't know about you, but I'm starving." *If we're eating, we don't have to talk.*

"Hmm, I thought all the cookies I bought were gone. Mrs. Baldwin must have saved some back. I'll take a chicken leg."

Victoria removed her fur-lined gloves and dug in the white parchment paper covered bowl full of chicken and found a leg. She pulled out a thigh for herself.

He looked at her and lifted an eyebrow. "Will we be fighting over the dark meat of the chicken?"

She wasn't sure if he was teasing or not, but she answered as if he was. "Not until we're down to the last piece, then I'll switch to the wings. I like them almost as much as I like the thighs."

Taking a big bite of the thigh, she felt her hunger already subsiding. The chicken was good, still crispy, not too salty. She was surprised since Andrew had said Mrs. Baldwin was not a good cook. The chicken was not as good as hers, but as hungry as she was, it tasted wonderful.

"So, tell me about yourself, Victoria. Only so much information can be put in a wire. They are too expensive."

She swallowed the meat in her mouth worried about the big lie she was about to tell him. "I'm twenty-four. I'm a widow but was only married for a few months. My husband was a sailor and except for our wedding night, I never saw him again. We had a whirlwind romance. He literally swept me off my feet. We met the end of August, married the first of September and he was gone the second."

"How did he die?"

"He fell overboard and was never recovered."

He reached over and squeezed her knee. "I'm sorry for your loss."

After practicing the lie on the train, it became easier to tell and she almost believed it herself. "You know, it's odd now. The courtship and marriage were so fast, because he was a sailor, I guess, that I don't really mourn him. I barely knew him."

"That happens sometimes, and it's nothing to feel ashamed of."

"Thank you. I just wanted you to understand why I'm not wearing black now. I figured I was starting a new life and that included leaving the old life behind."

He nodded. "I understand that. Now what else do we have in the basket?"

She smiled, knowing she'd have to prepare a lot of food to feed this man. Handing him a roast beef sandwich, she asked, "How many live on the ranch? Just the three of you?"

"No, ten men work for me. You'll meet them at dinner tonight, which you'll be cooking, by the way."

She nodded. "I'd wondered if I'd be cooking tonight. So there will be fourteen people total? I assume the men have great appetites."

"Yes, they all work hard and need a lot of food."

I did some of the cooking at the orphanage. Was cooking for forty children and fifteen members of the staff, the same as cooking for these men? "I'll try to remember that as I cook."

"I'm sure Mrs. Baldwin will help you with the amounts needed."

"Do you and your men like sweets? Cookies, cakes and such?"

His eyes lit up, and he grinned. "Do we ever? We only get them if I remember to buy some at the mercantile. Do you bake?"

"I do. I'm pretty good at it, if I do say so myself."

Andrew continued to smile. "I'm looking forward to your first efforts."

"I must see what you have available in the supplies. When do you do your shopping?"

"Saturdays. I did it before I picked you up, so I'm afraid you will have to wait until next week if I don't have the ingredients you need."

"Was your wife a baker?" She took the last bite of her chicken and when she was done, she tossed the bone out to the side as she'd watched him do.

He got quiet for a moment. "Yes, Elise loved to make cookies. When Suse could barely stand on a chair, she stood with her mother, and they made hand cookies. Do you know what those are?"

She nodded, remembering the times she'd made them with Margie over the years. The thought of Margie brought tears to her eyes, and she looked away. "Yes, I know how to make hand cookies. Perhaps Susannah would like to make them with me? Well, if your wife was a baker, I bet most, if not all the ingredients I need, to make cookies or a couple of cakes will be in your pantry. Maybe even in time for dinner."

His smile was back. "I'd like that. We all would."

"What time do you normally have dinner?"

He slapped the reins on the horses' butts and they lifted their heads. He did it again and again until they were running. "Usually at six, but we understand it might be a little later today while you find your way around the kitchen. On the back porch, is a triangle, when you're ready for us to come in for meals, you just run the rod around the inside of that triangle and the noise will bring us running whether for meals or for an emergency."

Victoria held on to her hat while the horses ran. He'd been doing this on and off the entire way. She thought he was probably in a hurry to get home to his young daughter.

He turned under an arch that said Mayfield Ranch, on to a long driveway. Victoria checked the watch on her wrist and saw about one hour and forty-five minutes had passed since leaving Golden City.

"It took us less time than you estimated."

He grinned. "I was in a hurry to get home to Suse. I can't wait for you to meet her. She holds my heart and is my world."

"I can't wait to meet her either." She settled her hands in her lap so he wouldn't see them shake even with her fur-lined gloves on.

"Do you know what you want for dinner tonight?"

"I don't know. You'll have to discuss that with Mrs. Baldwin."

"Yes, of course. Tell me about all the many buildings I see. The only one I can identify is the barn, because it's the biggest and it's painted red."

"The buildings to the left of the yard in front of the house, which is the large brown building in front, are the chicken house, ice house, and smokehouse. The outhouse is behind the main house. To the right are the bunkhouse, fore-man's cottage, and rabbit hutches. Back by the barn are the corrals and the hay shed."

"My goodness, but the ranch is quite large. If I bring you lunch in the barn, it will be cold by the time I reach you."

He laughed. "You won't have to bring me lunch. I'll come running with the rest of them when you ring that triangle. Also, on the porch outside the back door of the kitchen you'll find basins and pails. Those must have warm water in them before all meals. The men need to wash before they come inside to eat. Mrs. Baldwin will show you."

"Thank goodness for Mrs. Baldwin. I hope you mean to keep her around. I'll need all the help I can get, especially in the beginning."

"I have no intention of ever letting Mrs. Baldwin go. She was Elise's nanny and will stay until after Suse marries. Then Mrs. Baldwin will go with Suse."

He became quiet and the muscle in his jaw pulsed with each grind of his teeth.

"I'm sorry. I know Elise has not been gone that long."

He shrugged. "It doesn't matter. She'll always be with me and I'll always love her. You should know that and don't expect me to love you." He sat up straight and looked directly into her eyes. "I can't and I won't try."

As far as Victoria was concerned that sentiment was perfectly all right with her. "Fine. I comprehend completely. I ask that you can appreciate if I feel the same way."

He nodded. "We understand one another. Good. Very good."

He pulled up in front of the house. He set the brake and then came around and helped Victoria to the ground. Then he grabbed her bags out of the back with one hand and put the other at her waist to guide her in.

She couldn't believe how much of a gentleman he was. *Would he always be that way.*

Just as they walked up the flat stone path from the gate in the white picket fence to the porch, the door opened.

A small blonde little girl ran out.

"Daddy!"

She slowed down for the steps and took them one at a time with both feet on the step before moving on to the next. When she reached the bottom, she jumped into her father's arms.

Squatting, he caught her up into a tight hug.

"Miss me, Suse?"

She nodded fast. "Um hum. I did. Always miss you. Every day."

"I know, baby, but Daddy has to work. I brought someone for you to meet. This is Victoria. She's Daddy's new wife and will live with us from now on."

The little girl had the same big green eyes as her father. With her pale skin and those emerald eyes, she would be a heartbreaker when she grew up.

Susannah shook her head. "No want Toria." She squirmed.

Andrew put her down.

She ran off into the house, stopped and peeked around the door.

Andrew gazed at Victoria with a tilt to his head, lifted eyebrows and a frown. "I'm sorry. She doesn't mean that."

Victoria shook her head. "For now, she means it, and we can acknowledge that feeling. I was a governess for over three years and know a little about children and their moods. She's afraid she'll lose your attention because of me. The only way to put her at ease is to give her some extra attention now. I can do that and she'll get used to me."

Andrew looked from her to Susannah. "I'll let you do as you say. I want her to accept you."

"Maybe I can bribe her with a cookie or two." Victoria raised her voice so the child could hear. "Or maybe she'd like to help me make cookies. Would you like that, Susannah?"

The little girl shrugged.

Since she didn't flat out say *no*, Victoria thought that was a win for her side. Susannah wasn't indifferent to baking with her.

"Let's go meet Mrs. Baldwin."

Victoria entered and looked around at the house that was now her home. She was pleased. The parlor where they'd entered had natural walls of wood but it was varnished and the wood was light colored.

The furniture was done in shades of blue, the sofa in a light floral print with a pretty blue flower that she didn't recognize and the chairs in a deep, solid blue. The curtains matched the print on the sofa but were in a light cotton material.

One wall contained bookshelves on the lower half and a lovely painting of what looked like the ranch itself, with the purple mountains in the background, hung above the shelves. The sky was just as beautiful a blue as she'd seen on the way to the ranch today.

Andrew led the way down the hall to the kitchen, carrying Susannah. She passed a dining room on one side and what looked like his office on the other.

In the kitchen, a heavyset woman of average height stood at the stove, stirring something.

She set down the spoon on what must have been a cold burner and turned toward them. "I heard you drive up. Suse was so excited. I let her come out to you."

"I never tire of her greetings, whether I've been gone an hour or all day." He hugged his daughter again. "Nora, this is Victoria, my wife. This is Nora Baldwin, my housekeeper and all-round house help. She cleans the house and does the cooking, and takes care of Suse until now. I don't know what I'd do without her. You will ease her burden."

Victoria stepped forward and extended her right hand. "I'm so pleased to meet you, Mrs. Baldwin. Tell me what is it you have cooking in the big pot? It smells wonderful."

"Chili...for supper."

She looked at Andrew, who was smiling at Suse, and back to Mrs. Baldwin. "I don't believe I've ever had that dish before. What is in it?"

The older woman smiled and stirred the pot. "Cubes of

beef, beans, tomatoes, spices, all in the proper proportions. That's it. Then you let it simmer all day and stir occasionally so the food doesn't stick to the bottom of the pan. You'll get the hang of it. I'll give you the recipe."

Victoria looked again to Andrew for guidance.

He set down his daughter. "You'll start doing the cooking to help Nora out. Your main job will be caring for Suse. We'll talk more about the rest of your chores later."

The little girl hugged her Daddy's leg and stared at Victoria with a thumb in her mouth.

That will be one thing I work on changing. She's too old to be sucking her thumb. The next thing will be getting her father to love me before I tell him I'm expecting. I know I said I'd be find with him not loving me, but I know Emily was right and having him love me is the only way I, and my baby, will be safe.

CHAPTER FOUR

"Come with me, and I'll show you to the bedroom."

Victoria swallowed hard and took a deep breath. "Very good."

Back at the front door, he picked up her bags and headed up the stairs.

"Two of the four bedrooms are empty. Suse is in the one across from us at the end of the hall."

He walked down to the bedroom on the right.

Victoria followed him in awe. The house was beautiful. All of it natural wood, varnished to bring out the grain. The hall was wide, and the floor covered in a blue carpet of Eastern design, down the middle, leaving about a foot of the natural wood showing on either side.

"Your home is lovely."

"My wife designed and decorated it. You can change whatever you don't like."

"I can't imagine changing anything. So far, everything I've seen has been lovely."

He entered the room and held open the door for her.

The first thing she saw was a large portrait of a beautiful, blonde woman with big blue eyes. *She must be Elise, his dead wife.* Victoria closed her eyes for a moment. *How long will I have to look at her every day and be reminded of his loss and my deception?*

The bedroom was the only room she'd seen so far that had a masculine touch. The colors were still blue, but all dark and plain. The bed was covered in a patchwork quilt with squares from the curtains in the parlor and the curtains here. Other squares in different patterns, but all in various shades of the deep blue, were also in the quilt.

The bed was wood framed. It looked like the same wood they built the house from. The curved headboard and footboard were plain except for their shape.

Nightstands, the bureau, tallboy dresser and commode were made from the wood matching the bed. Two windows were across from the entry door with a fireplace in between them.

"Hangers are in the closet." He pointed at the door across the room from the bed. "The two middle drawers in the bureau and the top drawers in the dresser are empty for your use."

"I won't need that much space."

"Doesn't matter. They are there if you want them. I'll let you unpack. When you're done, come back to the kitchen, and we'll discuss the rest of the chores you'll be responsible for."

"All right. I'll be down in about twenty minutes, or before."

"Take your time. I have to check on the animals, so I'll be awhile myself." He turned and left the room.

Victoria looked after him, noticed how well his shoulders filled out his shirt and then caught herself. *Be careful, Victoria. He just lost his wife and won't be looking for a new love. His world is his daughter, and if he didn't need you to care for her, he wouldn't have married you or anyone else.*

Putting her clothes away didn't take long. She'd need to iron her dresses, but she could do that tomorrow or perhaps tonight after dinner. Victoria really wasn't looking forward to tonight and was searching for any excuse to put off having sex with Andrew. Though she found him attractive, she remembered Oliver and the rape. Was all sex like that? Would she be frightened, like she was when Oliver had taken her? What if she was showing more than she thought? Could he tell she was expecting? Would he find her hips too wide? She did have wide hips and a large bottom. Since she'd gotten in the family way, her breasts had gotten bigger, were they too big now?

She finished putting away her clothes and toiletries, refreshed herself from the trip and then headed down to the kitchen. Before she got there, she heard laughter. Little girl giggles and deep male chuckles. When she entered, Andrew stopped laughing and stared at her. She saw the hunger in his eyes and knew there was no way she could put off having relations tonight. Resigning herself to the fact, she was determined to make the best of the rest of the day and evening.

"Do you mind if I look in the pantry for the makings for a cake? I have time to bake one for dessert."

"Of course. Then we'll talk about tomorrow's chores."

"About that. I was raised in an orphanage. We had a few cows and chickens. I know how to milk a cow and gather eggs." She walked to the door on the wall next to the stove. Entering, she found cupboards above a counter with bins underneath. The bins held flour, sugar, and cornmeal. In the cupboards were canned goods, coffee, and cocoa powder and all the ingredients needed to make a cake. She smiled. Elise definitely liked to bake.

Victoria gathered the needed items and took them out,

setting them on the counter next to the sink. Then she joined Andrew at the table.

He sat at the head. Susannah was in her highchair on his left and Victoria sat on his right. "I'm certain I will enjoy your cake. That's a rare treat around here. He smiled and motioned to the far chair. "You'll be sitting at the other end of the table when we take meals."

"I noticed the table is large enough to seat approximately twenty people. I assume that means the men eat with us."

"Yes, it does." He narrowed his eyes. "Do you have a problem with that?"

She shook her head. "Not at all. It's just, when I was a governess, I ate with Margie in the kitchen not with the master and mistress in the dining room."

"Ah." He gave a slight nod. "We don't have that kind of delineation of classes here in the West. Everyone is equal."

Susannah said, "Daddy, I ride my pony now."

"No, Suse. I'm talking to Victoria right now."

The little girl kicked the legs of her highchair and pounded on the tray. "Ride now."

"No, and don't you take that tone of voice with me, young lady. For that you're going to your room." Andrew's voice deepened, he stood and picked up Savannah from her highchair.

"Andrew," said Victoria. "She's only two. She's jealous of me."

"She needs to learn to be respectful, and she's old enough to start that lesson." He took his daughter's hand.

She refused to walk and sat on the floor.

Andrew scooped up his wailing child and carried her out of the room.

Nora nodded after them. "She's normally a good child, but she's afraid she'll lose her father like she did her mama."

"I know. I understand that. She just needs time to learn

I'm not taking her Daddy away. That I'm here to stay with her and him."

"She'll come around."

Victoria stood. "Would you show me where the mixing bowls are and the cake pans are? I thought I'd bake a cake for dessert."

"If you're making 'em, you better make two. Those boys will not be satisfied with a little slice of cake."

"True. How many cake pans do you have?"

Nora got a rueful smile on her face. "Six. Elise always made three when she baked. She loved to bake, that girl."

Victoria saw the tear before Nora wiped it away with her dishtowel. "You miss her, don't you? You all do. I'm not trying to take her place."

"No one can take her place," said Andrew, entering the kitchen. He poured a cup of coffee and then sat back at the table.

Victoria resumed her seat next to him, folding her hands in her lap. She tried not to feel upset but to be understanding. She found it difficult not to feel sorry for herself. She just wanted a home and a safe place. Her intentions were never to cause anyone pain. "What else did you want to tell me about my chores?" She held up a hand and ticked off her fingers. "Milk the cow, gather the eggs and take care of Susannah."

"You'll also help Nora with the laundry and the cooking and the ironing." He took a swig of coffee. "But no matter what, you take care of Suse first."

"Speaking of laundry, I need to get it off the line." Nora picked up the basket by the back door and headed out. "If you'll both excuse me for a bit."

"Of course, Nora. Do you need some help?" asked Victoria.

"No, I'm fine but thanks for offering." The older woman

smiled and if Victoria wasn't mistaken, a bit of sympathy in the smile crossed her face.

Victoria returned her gaze to Andrew. "I will always take care of Susannah first. I'm good with children, though it may take me a little longer with her. She's very attached to you and rightly so. I'm afraid she won't accept me easily."

He leaned back in his chair. "Then you'll just have to keep after her. She's just a little bit of a thing."

"With a very good set of lungs." Victoria ducked her head and smiled, but kept her gaze on Andrew.

"That she does." He looked heavenward and smiled. "That she does."

Overhead they could still hear Susannah hollering at her father. "Daddeeeee! Daddeeeee!"

She took a deep breath, not sure how he would react to her giving him advice. "You should check on her in a little bit and try to calm her. It's not good for her to scream like that for any length of time. I know many parents would just let them cry themselves out, but I don't believe that's the best way with a child. I believe it builds resentment."

"You should go to her," said Andrew. "Maybe you can get her to calm down."

Victoria slowly shook her head. "I don't know, it's too soon. She—"

"Needs to get used to you and know you will be there for her. Try it. See what happens."

Despite her misgivings, Victoria stood and headed out of the room. When Andrew came with her, it surprised her.

"You...you're coming, too?"

"I love my daughter. I don't want her in such distress either, but I want her to know that you will be there for her and me. If you can't calm her, I'll come in. But she needs to realize she is not in charge, we are and we make the rules."

Victoria ducked her head just a bit. "You are correct." She headed out of the room followed by Andrew.

She went up the stairs with him beside her and stopped at the end of the hall across from their bedroom.

Victoria took a deep breath and opened the door.

Andrew stayed in the hallway.

Victoria left the door open a bit so he could hear. In the room was a crib, where Susannah stood, lots of toys and a small single bed.

Susannah turned and sat with her back to Victoria. Then she sniffled. "G'way, not want you."

Victoria sat on the floor next to the crib. "I'm all you have right now, baby girl. I'm really not so bad. You and I can have fun together. We can play and make cookies for your Daddy."

A few minutes later, Susannah turned and looked around. She held out a hand toward the door and opened her mouth wide.

"If you scream again, I'll leave and you'll spend the rest of the afternoon here by yourself. If you don't, you can come back downstairs with me to see your father."

The child startled at Victoria's voice and then sniffled again but did not yell. Susannah raised her arms.

Victoria stood, picked her up and carried her down the stairs. She heard Andrew's boots as he hurried back to the kitchen.

As soon as she and the little girl entered the room, Susannah wiggled down and ran to her father.

Victoria walked to the table and sat next to Andrew.

Susannah stopped by his chair. "We ride pony now?"

He shook his head. "Maybe tomorrow."

She opened her mouth wide.

He stared down at his daughter. "If you scream again, you'll go right back upstairs, and I won't let Victoria come for you. Understand?"

Susannah closed her mouth and nodded.

"If you're a good girl, I'll take you to your pony after Victoria finishes baking her cakes."

He looked over at Victoria, eyes twinkling.

She smiled. "I see you remember what I was about to do."

Nora came in the back door carrying a basket full of clothes. "I swear most of these are that child's. She must change her clothes ten times a day, but I never know which pile in her room is the dirty ones and which are clean, so I wash them all. I almost wish she hadn't learned to dress herself."

Victoria lifted her brows. "That's very good for a child her age. Dressing herself, I mean." She stood, noticing that Nora had put out a huge mixing bowl and six round cake pans. "Nora said I should make three cakes."

Andrew nodded and grinned. "Unless you want to make four."

"Four cakes! Good grief, how much food do these men eat."

He laughed.

She liked the sound. It was deep and rumbled through her, reminding her of a younger man's laugh. A man without responsibilities or worries.

"They eat a lot. You'll see."

Nora carried the clothes out of the kitchen.

Victoria leaned over and touched Susannah's hand "If you take your thumb out of your mouth, you can help me bake some cakes."

The little girl took her thumb out of her mouth and shook her head.

Victoria smiled and lifted one brow. "You can lick the bowl."

Andrew grinned. "What about her Daddy? Does he get to lick the bowl, too?"

Victoria laughed. "I'll make sure to leave enough for two."

"Sounds good to me. What do you say, Suse? Want to help bake a cake?"

She thought for a moment and then nodded quickly. "I help."

"Let me gather the ingredients and bring them over here so you can put them in the bowl. Then we'll wash our hands before we prepare the food." Victoria got a basin off the porch and poured first hot and then cold water in it until it was just warm. She didn't want Susannah to burn her hands.

She help the child wash and then Victoria washed her hands.

After they were both clean Victoria placed all the ingredients already in containers in the bowl and unloaded it at the kitchen table, and then she got six eggs, all the flour and sugar she would need in separate bowls. Once everything was gathered she turned to Susannah. "Come stand here on the bench between me and the table. I'll add the ingredients to the bowl and you can stir them. How's that?"

"Okay." Suse clambered off her father's lap and lifted her arms to Victoria.

She picked her up and set her on the bench.

Together, with Victoria adding ingredients and Suse stirring, they mixed the batter for the chocolate cakes. Victoria gave it the final one hundred strokes required to make the batter smooth. Then she poured it into the six cake pans. She gave Andrew the big stirring spoon and the child a soup spoon, then set the bowl between them.

Then she walked to the stove and tested the oven temperature by holding her hand inside the oven. It was ready for the cakes, and she put them in on the middle rack of the large oven, before joining her new family at the table. The magnificent, imported stove dominated the already large kitchen and matched the grandness and beauty of the entire house. Being able to cook on such a stove gave her a thrill.

Twenty-five minutes later Victoria tested the doneness of the cake layers. Finding them fully baked, she pulled two from the oven and repeated the process until all six cakes were on the counter, cooling.

"Andrew, keep Susannah over there. The oven is very hot, and she may not remember that."

"I've got her." He picked up his daughter and held her until Victoria came back to the table.

"How long before they're ready to eat?" Andrew licked his lips.

Victoria followed the progress of his tongue over his full lips and found her mouth open.

He grinned and then winked.

She snapped back, realizing she'd been ogling her husband and knew she was probably red as an apple.

"They need to cool and that will take about an hour or hour and a half. Then I need to frost them. Thank goodness Nora is here. I couldn't do the cakes and dinner, too, without her help. I'll have one ready for you about," she looked at her wristwatch. "Four o'clock."

Four o'clock came around, and the back door opened. Andrew entered she assumed coming from the barn. He walked into the kitchen, rubbing his hands together. "I'm ready for some of that cake now, wife."

Wife! Two could play at this. She stopped kneading the dough for second batch of bread. The first batch might rise enough to bake for dinner, but she wasn't counting on it. She'd make biscuits so they were sure to have bread with the meal. "Very well, *husband*. Sit and I'll get you a cup of coffee and a small piece of cake. I don't want you or Suse ruining your dinners."

"She can share with me. She just needs a small glass of milk."

"What about you, Nora? Will you have cake with us?"

"Of course." She sat at the table.

Victoria brought everyone their drinks, then cake, and she did cut a tiny piece for Susannah.

Once she was seated, everyone began to eat. She took a bite and was pleased with the flavor. She ate part of her slice and then lost her appetite waiting for Andrew to tell her what he thought.

He ate slowly and washed down the dessert with a swig of black coffee.

"Well? What do you think?"

He took another bite, swallowed and smiled. "It's great. Can't wait to try your other efforts."

Her body relaxed. "I'm glad you like it. I might not be much of a cook, but Nora will help me with that. I am an excellent baker." Victoria touched the little girl's hand. "Susannah will help me, won't you?"

She nodded. "I Suse."

"All right. Suse will help me bake cookies tomorrow. Yes?"

Suse nodded so fast she moved on her daddy's lap. "Yup. I help."

Victoria grinned from ear to ear. *One down, now if I can just win her father over.*

CHAPTER FIVE

New York City, December 28, 1870
   The Thomas home

"Where is she, David? Tell me. She's been gone for three weeks and I know you know where she went."

David Thomas sat across the breakfast from his wife, Mildred.

"Who are you talking about?"

"You know perfectly well. Victoria. Where did she go? I want that child. I won't have any bastard taking what is rightfully Margery's."

David put his fork down, his appetite gone and pushed his plate away. "Why would I know where she went?"

"I saw you say goodbye and send her on her way. I know you know where she went from here."

"I haven't any idea what you're talking about, and even if I did, I'd never tell you. You're a witch, Mildred, and I wish I'd never met you much less married you."

"Oh, but you are glad for my Margery. Yes, *my* Margery. She's not yours, you know."

"I've always known, but I married you anyway. Witch that you are." He threw down his napkin and stood. "We're done here." He turned and walked out.

"Don't you turn your back on me, you bastard. You hear me? I'm still talking to you." She stood and ran after him, jumping on his back and scratching his face.

He threw her off and she landed on the floor. "Stay there, if you know what's good for you." David touched a hand to his face. "Don't you ever come near me, or Margie, again. If I see you even talking to her, I will throw you out of the house with nothing but the clothes on your back and none of my friends will help you. Understand?"

"You can't do that. I'll take Margie away. I'll—"

He stood ramrod straight, his hands fisted at his sides. "You'll do nothing because no judge in this town will issue a custody order against me. Now, do you understand?"

The anger on her face was unmistakable. "Yes, I understand."

He was sure, if she had a dagger, she'd bury it in his back. From now on, he'd have to be on his guard for that very occurrence.

———

Outside Brides for the West, Monday, January 2, 1871

Mildred stopped outside the green door in the brownstone. If anyone knew where that little witch had gone, it would be Emily Johnson, David's friend. Mildred would bet her bottom dollar that she'd found a husband for the she-devil and David had made all the payments necessary.

She entered the office.

Emily looked up and swallowed hard.

Oh yes, Mildred was definitely right, but she'd have to play it well. She knew Emily would not reveal Victoria's location easily.

"Emily, how are you?" she asked sweetly.

"Fine. What can I do for you, Mildred? Surely you're not looking for a new husband." She laughed at her little joke.

Mildred chuckled. "Oh, no, not at all." *I'll tell the truth, or what sounds like the truth. She won't be expecting that.* "Actually, I'm looking for my governess. She left without her last paycheck and I want to see that she gets it. Victoria Coleman?"

"I don't remember anyone by that name. Let me look at my records." She thumbed through the files in the cabinet behind her desk. "Nothing for that name. Would she have been using a different name, perhaps? Often, these young women have found themselves in desperate circumstances and use another name."

Mildred thought for a moment. What name would she have used? Then it hit her. "Could you have someone named Margie Coleman?"

"Let me see." She thumbed through again. "Ah, yes, I do. If you'll give me the check, I'll see that she gets it."

"Just give me the address, I'll send it myself."

"I'm afraid I can't do that. Part of my service is complete anonymity so they cannot be found."

Mildred was not deterred. She'd just break-in tonight and get the information she needed. "I see. Well, that's all right. I didn't bring her check with me but I'll return with it so you can get it to her."

Emily raised an eyebrow. "Very good. I will see you then."

"Yes, you will." Mildred turned and left the office.

————

Emily watched her go and knew Mildred would be back when Emily wasn't around to stop her. She took Victoria's file with her when she left that night.

The next morning, as soon as she opened her office, Emily knew Mildred had returned. She looked on her desk for the dummy file she'd made and saw it was gone. Emily smiled.

She filed Victoria's real papers in the cabinet and cleaned up the mess Mildred had left.

The next day she walked into the office and saw it was a mess again. She ran to the file cabinet and looked for Victoria's folder. It was gone. Now Mildred knew where she'd gone.

Emily wondered what she should do and sent a message to David for him to meet her as soon as possible. She sent it with one of her best girls, Jean Simon, with instructions she was to give it to no one but David.

David appeared about fifteen minutes after Jean had returned.

He rushed in the door. "What's the matter?"

"Mildred was here, asking for Victoria. I thought I'd put her off the scent when she took the dummy folder I made up, but she returned last night and took the real folder. She knows where Victoria is."

David punched a fist into his other hand. "That explains why she was in such a hurry to get out of the house this morning. Told me she would stay with her mother for a few weeks. It delighted me not to have to put up with her. We must wire Victoria and warn her."

"Yes, my thoughts exactly."

"I'll do it on my way back home. I don't like to leave Margie with just cook to watch her, even with Mildred supposedly gone. She wants me to drop my guard."

"Understood. I'm so sorry, David."

"This situation is not your fault, Emily. Mildred is a sly person and has been honing her craft for years."

Emily let out a long breath. "I know, but that fact doesn't make me feel any better because I knew, deep down, that she was a wily person."

He gave her a hug. "Don't worry. Victoria will be warned and will take the appropriate actions."

————

Saturday, January 7, 1871

Victoria, Andrew and Suse headed into town on a beautiful January morning. Victoria had been with Andrew for about a month and was afraid she was showing already. She was four months pregnant and terrified because, although Andrew was kind, she knew he was not in love with her. Not yet.

Unfortunately, she was now in love with her husband and daughter. Suse was now comfortable with Victoria, allowed her to comfort her, wanted goodnight kisses, and stories from her—all the things a daughter wants from her mother.

Andrew had not forced her to have relations that first night. He'd realized she was exhausted from the trip and only held her. That was probably the second nicest thing any man had ever done for her. He actually thought about what she needed rather than his own needs.

She knew she'd started falling in love with her husband when she saw him with his daughter. He was so gentle with her and yet firm as well. And Suse absolutely adored him. Victoria understood that feeling for it was building within her.

The next night he'd made gentle love to her. Nothing was hurried about it and she'd loved him a little more then. Now, she looked forward as much as he did to making love each night, and especially to the cuddling afterward.

She discovered making love with her husband was nothing like the rape she'd suffered at Oliver's hands, for which she was eternally grateful.

Now after a month, she was happy with her new life. Even if Andrew didn't love her, he seemed to respect her, and that was all she could ask.

They arrived in town for their regular Saturday shopping. As they entered the Golden City Mercantile, the owner, Ed Swanson, greeted them. The store was packed, as usual, with all the ranchers and farmers doing their weekly shopping.

"Andrew, Victoria and little Suse. How are you all today?" He tweaked Suse's cheek.

She smiled and ducked her head into her daddy's shoulder.

Andrew shifted Suse in his arms so he could shake hands with Ed. "We're good, how are you?"

"Finer than frog's hair." He chuckled.

Victoria laughed, having never heard that particular phrase before.

"I have something for you, Victoria. It came in on Tuesday, and Jed knew you'd be in today, so he gave it to me to deliver to you." Ed pulled an envelope out of his apron pocket and handed it to her. "Here you go. One wire delivered to you, as promised."

Victoria knew she paled. Only one person would send her a wire and it wouldn't be with good news. She took the envelope with shaking hands. "Thank you. I'll open it later."

Andrew lifted a brow but said nothing.

She would have to tell him everything now, and she was afraid he would never forgive her and would turn her out. She couldn't blame him. She'd deceived him. The fact she'd been protecting herself and her unborn baby wouldn't matter.

She probably should tell him now, so he could leave her

now rather than have to come back. But she decided he'd have to return anyway to bring her clothes, so it would wait until the way home or until they were alone. It wouldn't do to fight in front of Suse.

Putting the envelope in her reticule, she took out her list to fill at the mercantile.

"Aren't you going to read it?" asked Ed. "It might be important."

Victoria shook her head. "I've waited this long to read it, it will wait a little longer. I want Andrew and I to be alone when the missive is read."

Andrew smiled.

Ed frowned. "Well, darn. I've been wondering what was in that since Jed gave it to me on Tuesday. We don't get many wires that come in, ya know."

She smiled.

"Thanks for delivering the wire. We'll do our shopping now." Andrew put his hand at Victoria's waist and guided her away from Ed. "We'll discuss the wire later."

Knots filled her stomach and she thought sure she'd throw up. "Yes, I planned on it. Perhaps on the way home. I must see what it says and decide if we should discuss it in front of Suse."

"'Cuss what?" asked Suse.

"Nothing, baby girl." Andrew gave her a kiss on the forehead. "Let's get our stuff and get out of this madhouse."

"We should really consider coming to town some other day than Saturday. Everyone from out-of-town, including us, comes in on Saturday."

"You're right. Maybe we should come on Friday. I'll consider it."

Perhaps since he's being so agreeable, he'll not be too upset when I tell him what I really am and why I married him. "Thank you."

"For what?"

"For considering my opinion and taking it into account." *We are starting to get to know each other so well and it will be hard to leave him and Suse, if that should be his choice.* The lump in her throat expanded and she could hardly swallow.

He nodded. "I want us to be considerate of each other."

"I do, as well."

Two hours later they were on their way home with the wagon full of groceries and grain for the animals.

"Are you going to read the wire?" Andrew slapped the reins on the horse's butts.

"Yes, I suppose I should." She pulled the envelope from her bag and tore it open.

Victoria

Mildred has your location and is on her way. Watch yourself.

David

Her stomach clenched and her hands started to shake. She read the wire again. Mildred had found her. What would she do now? She read it to Andrew.

"So who is Mildred?"

"My previous employer's wife."

"Why would she be coming here?"

"It's a long story. Perhaps we should wait until we get home."

He looked down at Suse, who was asleep with her head on his lap and her feet on Victoria's.

"Sounds like we should discuss it now, and we have two hours to do it."

Her stomach roiling, Victoria folded the wire and replaced it in her bag, then clasped her hands to keep them from shaking. "You won't like it. I'll tell you that right now."

"Let me be the judge of that. Begin."

She gazed at him through her lashes, her head still down cast. "I guess the first place to start is to tell you, I've never been married, and I'm pregnant."

He breathed deeply and closed his eyes. "I figured that out already, the pregnant part. Go on."

"My best friend's husband raped me. That's why I was not a virgin when we married. My employer, David Thomas, helped me to escape, because his wife thought we were having an affair, and that the baby I carry is his. It's not. Mr. Thomas was never anything but kind to me. He gave me the money to get the clothes I needed to live here." She wouldn't tell him the amount Mr. Thomas had given her. She still might need it to live. "Apparently, Mrs. Thomas has decided to take matters into her own hands and is coming here. What she expects to get from me, I don't know."

Andrew was quiet.

Her eyes filled with tears. "I'm sorry, Andrew. I never intended to hurt you or to be anything but a good wife. I'll understand if you want me to leave."

"I don't want you to leave, but I wish I'd known the truth before now."

She looked up at him, her eyes glistening unshed tears. "Would it have made a difference? Would you have let me stay, anyway?"

He turned toward her, his eyes narrowed and his mouth in a frown. "We'll never know now, will we?"

She looked down at her lap. "No, I suppose we won't. Do you want me to move to the spare room? I can appreciate why you won't want me in your bed."

His gaze never left her. "Victoria. I have no intention of anything changing. I understand why you went to such lengths, but I need some time to think about it. For now, I want nothing to change."

He got quiet, and when he spoke, it was a whisper she barely heard above the din of the horses' hooves on the dirt road.

"The son of the richest man in town raped my sister,

Susannah. He nearly beat her to death, but everyone said it was her fault. She must have asked for it. I know she did nothing except kept turning the man down when he wanted to court her, and that attack is what she got in return. She couldn't live with what everyone was saying and with the looks she got from the men. Susannah ended up taking her own life rather than live like that, and I didn't stop it. I didn't save her."

Her throat tightened, her heart breaking for the young man Andrew was then. "What could you have done? Killing the man would only have put you in jail, and your sister would have had no one to protect her. She might have died sooner or been attacked again by some man who thought she would let him have relations with her for whatever reason. Nothing you could have done would have changed the outcome for your sister. Believe me, I considered it myself."

He reached over and placed a hand on her knee. "I'm glad you didn't."

"So am I. But what do we do now? I'm expecting in about five months. I know you lost your wife and child last year, so are you ready to take on a woman and a child that isn't yours? Are you ready to accept my child, even knowing how it was conceived?"

"Do you accept it?"

Her hand lay against her stomach. "Of course. This child is innocent. It had nothing to do with the way I conceived it and should not be held responsible for it."

He nodded. "I agree."

She widened her eyes in surprise. "You do?"

The horses began to slow due to the incline which though not particularly steep, was still difficult for them with a full wagon to pull. Andrew slapped the reins again to get them moving. "I do. I would have accepted Susannah's child, too, if she'd been with child. She died about two months after the attack, so I'll never know. I left Missouri then, moved here and bought my ranch. That was over ten years ago. About two years after I moved here, I met Elise and we married, about five years later we had Susannah, who we named after my sister. Elise didn't have any problems with Suse, but the second pregnancy was fraught with troubles."

She reached across Suse and placed her hand on his arm where it rested on his thigh. "I'm sorry for that, and that you lost your wife. I know you loved her, and I'm sorry she died."

"So am I, but now we have to figure out how to keep you safe. I don't believe the woman on her way here means you well."

Victoria returned her hand to her lap and looked over the horse's heads to the land beyond. It was a wild land, open and, except for the occasional cluster of trees, looked barren in the winter they currently had. Now it was covered with snow the only dirt to be seen along the road they traveled. "No, I can guarantee she means me harm, but I don't know what kind or what she plans on doing to achieve her goals."

He stiffened. His back now ramrod straight. "Don't think my attitude means I accept what you did. I don't. You used me for your own ends, and I wasn't given a choice."

"Would you have married me knowing the truth?"

He didn't answer.

"See, that's what I thought. I needed the protection marriage could give me. I needed you and...I believe you needed me."

CHAPTER SIX

The rest of the trip home was done mostly in silence. Andrew wondered if Victoria was mulling over the same thoughts as he had.

What should I do? I can't let her go. She means more to me now than I thought possible. Maybe I love her, I don't know. My feelings for Victoria differ from those I had for Elise. And she's exactly what Suse needed. She's a well-behaved child now. No tantrums. When she gets angry and starts to scream, demanding things, Victoria takes her aside, talks to her, and the child returns to the sweet thing she usually is.

He looked over at her. She was hanging her head and appeared to be crying. He reached over and took her hand in his.

"I don't want you upset. It's not good for the baby. We'll figure things out. But I have to admit, I am angry and hurt. I thought we were building something between us and now I discover everything about you was a lie. How did you expect I would react? Or did you ever plan on telling me?"

She squeezed his hand. "I was hoping you would have

fallen in love with me before I told you. But that hasn't happened."

He removed his hand and put it back on the reins. "I don't know that will ever happen, but I can tell you I care for you. I would hope you care for me. I know you love Suse almost as much as I do." He looked down at his sleeping daughter. "She is my life. Everything I do, I do for her. That's why you're staying. I won't take another person she loves from her."

Victoria took a deep breath and nodded. "I understand. Thank you for not turning me away."

He nodded and directed his attention back to the horses. "I will never turn you away. You're safe with me."

———

Victoria was surprised at his generosity in letting her stay. He was giving her more than she'd hoped for and regardless of what he said, she still hoped that someday he would fall in love with her, as she had with him. He was more than kind to her and she would have missed his laugh, his teasing, the gentle way he was with Suse. Yet he was also firm with her without being cruel. How could she not have fallen in love with him?

She looked over at him, taking in every line on his beloved face, every wrinkle around those emerald eyes, and every laugh line on the sides of his mouth. She remembered those firm yet soft lips and wished she could feel them on her lips this instant.

Suse slept through this discussion between her parents. Yes, she was her parent and her mother. She would never willingly relinquish that role. This child was hers, and she couldn't love her more. Her beauty was already showing—her mother's face and her father's eyes.

Victoria looked at the portrait of Elise every day. Andrew still had it on their bedroom wall and yes, she was a beautiful woman. Suse looked just like her with her curly hair the color of corn silk, creamy skin and naturally pink cheeks. Victoria could brush the child's hair for hours if Suse would sit still for it, but she won't. Victoria was lucky to get the child's hair into a ponytail before she ran off to play with the new kittens in the barn.

Andrew dutifully waited for her and brought her back when he finished with his chores.

Soon she'd have new puppies to play with. Their dog, Daisy, was about to have her litter. Victoria thought it would be day now. She'd made the dog a bed behind the stove so the pups would be warm even when mama was away.

Andrew said that Daisy was a good mama. This would be her second litter and he would let Suse keep one as her dog. He would even let her choose which puppy to keep. He hoped one of them would choose her as well. The rest would be given away.

Why Victoria thought of all these normal things now, when her life was anything but normal, she didn't know. Maybe she needed to tell herself that her life was okay. Needed to reassure herself that she would be fine and Andrew would love her someday. Yet, as hard as she tried, she couldn't. She was afraid Andrew would never forgive her, and that he would always look at her as the woman who lied and roped him into marriage.

———

Finally at home, Victoria waited until Andrew set the brake and came around to her side, then she handed a still sleepy Suse to her father.

He took the child inside and came back for Victoria.

She had climbed into the back to hand the groceries down to him. After she'd handed him the last, she made her way down and was brushing the dust off her skirt when he returned.

"I would have helped you."

"I managed. Thank you, though."

"You're welcome, though I don't know for what." He grumbled the words.

She could tell he was not happy, but that was all right. She wasn't either.

The groceries needed putting away, and she didn't have time right now to talk. They'd done their talking in the wagon. Now, she had work to do.

Andrew left with the wagon to unload the grain.

Victoria and Suse walked into the kitchen.

"Suse, I want you to go up and play in your room until I get the groceries put away and we're ready for lunch."

"Okay." She ran off carrying her dolly.

Nora was in the kitchen just finishing the lunch dishes. "I save you all lunch. It's in the warming oven, but I detect some tension between you and Andrew. Care to elaborate?"

Victoria looked around for Andrew, and then told Nora everything.

"Ah, honey." Nora walked over and gave her a hug. "You've been through a lot, and Andrew will come around. I knew something was amiss when you never had your menses."

Victoria cocked her head and furrowed her brows. "But how? I figured Andrew saw the changes in my body."

Nora smiled. "I do the laundry, remember, and there were never any used rags or cloths."

She took a deep breath and leaned back against the counter next to Nora. "No, I guess there weren't. I should have known you'd suspect something. I should have been honest in the beginning, but I didn't believe Andrew would marry me and now...I just don't know. He says nothing will change, but he's angry, and I don't blame him."

"He'll get over his anger. He's a good man. You'll see, mark my words."

Suddenly, Daisy howled.

Victoria hurried to the stove and looked behind it. Daisy was in labor and there was one puppy part way out.

Victoria urged her on. "Come on, girl, you can do it."

"What do you see?" asked Nora from behind Victoria.

"There's one puppy part way out."

The dog whimpered, and the puppy slid out. Daisy twisted and started licking the puppy to remove the birthing sack. While she was doing this, another puppy started to exit her body.

This process went on for five puppies and then she was finally done. Victoria was glad she'd done it all herself as she hadn't looked forward to pulling the puppies out, though she would have. She'd done it before at the orphanage.

Andrew and Suse came in just after the puppies were finished being born.

He held Suse's hand. "What's going on? What are you doing behind the stove? Is Daisy having her pups?"

Victoria nodded and wiped the sweat from her head. "Yes, she did. Five of the little things. Suse come see." Victoria waved her daughter over.

"Puppies!" screamed Suse. She dropped her father's hand and ran to Victoria.

Victoria had to hold her back from picking up the puppies. "We need to let the puppies get a little older before we can hold them. But, if you're a good girl, you can watch them whenever you want."

Suse frowned at first. But when she heard she could watch them anytime, she perked up.

"Okay. I'll be good so I can."

Andrew lifted an eyebrow and looked over the top of Suse at Victoria, who sat on the floor. "Well, that didn't take long."

"No, except for the first one who is also the biggest. She popped them right out, one after the other. She's a good mama, immediately cleaned them and let them nurse."

Andrew cocked his head and gazed at her intently. "You're a good mother, too."

Victoria ducked her head and knew she blushed. "Thank you. That means a lot to me, coming from you."

"I only speak the truth."

Out of the corner of her eye, she saw Nora leave the room.

"Can you tell what the puppies are at this early age?"

"Let me see." He went around the stove to the other side. Carefully he picked up each puppy and turned it over. "This one is a boy. This is a girl. Boy. Girl. Girl. So, Suse, we need three girls' names and two boys' names. What do you think they should be?"

She looked closely the puppies and then pointed to each one as she named them. "That's Patches, 'cause of his black eye. That one is Sally, 'cause she gots yellow hair like my doll and dat's her name. That's Blackie, 'cause he's all black. That one is Daisy, 'cause she looks just like her mama."

Victoria rubbed her hand over Suse soft, blonde curls. "Do you think we should have two dogs named Daisy? It will get confusing. What if you call her Maisy, instead?"

The child cocked her head and pressed her lips together for a moment and then nodded. "Okay. Maisy. And that last one is Buttons 'cause she has buttons on her tummy."

"Those are very good names, sweet girl," said her Daddy.

"T'anks." Suse watched the puppies as they shakily found a nipple and began to nurse. Then she stood. "Bye, Toria. Bye, Daddy."

Victoria watched her go. "Stay in the house." She called

after her daughter. "When does she turn three? She just seems to grow so fast."

"I'm glad you mentioned it. I keep meaning to ask if you'll make her a special cake for her birthday, which is tomorrow."

She stood and put her hands on her hips. "And I'm only finding this out now? I don't have a present for her. I'll make a chocolate cake, it's her favorite, and spice cakes for the men, so her cake really will be special."

"Good, she'll like that."

"I was making clothes for her doll, but have only gotten them cut out. I'll sew one together tonight."

Andrew ran his hand through his hair. "I'm sorry. I should have told you before."

"It's all right. She's only three. She won't know any different."

"That's true. We didn't do anything last year. It was just another day, although I got her Sally...her doll."

Victoria smiled, picturing Suse asleep with Sally in her arms. "Yes, I am well-acquainted with Sally. She loves that doll."

"Well, it's good to know she likes something I did."

"You make it sound like she hasn't liked something you did. What would that be?"

"I took away her mother and baby brother."

All the air left Victoria's lungs. "I'm sure you had nothing to do with that. You have to know she couldn't have been helped more than she was. I'm sure the doctor did everything he possibly could."

"That's what he said. That sometimes these things just happen."

"And it's true. In some ways it frightens me...the thought of going through the birth. I know it hurts incredibly." She touched her stomach which was getting rounder. "But I can't wait to meet this little person. I don't care if it's a boy or a girl. All I know is that here they will be raised with love. I think Suse will be happy to have a brother or sister and will dote on the baby incessantly."

"You don't think she'll be jealous?"

"Maybe a little, but as long as we involve her in everything with the baby she'll be fine. She won't feel left out."

He furrowed his brows while observing her intently. "You've already thought of how having a baby in the house will be for her. You're amazing, you know that?"

Victoria smiled widely at his praise. "Thank you. Being a mother is all I've ever wanted to be. I never thought I would though, because I had found no one to marry, and I'm already an old maid or I was. Anyway, I put my energies into raising Margie, since her mother had no desire to do so."

"How can a mother have no desire for their own baby?"

"Mildred isn't exactly the motherly type, so Mr. Thomas... David...and I raised her. She only has him now, and he's not her father by blood, much as you'll be with this baby. He married Mildred because she was expecting and she was beautiful. She had him totally fooled as to the kind of woman she really is." Victoria picked some lint off her skirt and served them each a cup of coffee before continuing. "He hired me before the baby was born, and I raised Margie. She's three now, almost four, and he figured out she couldn't be his because Mildred was at least two months already pregnant when they got together. By the time he confronted her, all she did was laugh and tell him he was naïve."

He sat at the table, his hands circling the coffee cup, as though they were cold. "And this is the woman who is on her way here and means to do you harm?"

Victoria nodded, her stomach threatening to regurgitate the coffee she'd drank. "I believe she wants to kill me. She wants no other claims on David's fortune than Margie's. You see David is a very rich man. He owns half a dozen banks in

New York City and several in other cities as well. I can't think of any other reason she'd be coming."

"I believe you're correct. Nothing else makes sense, especially if her husband is as rich as you say he is."

Victoria shook her head, tears running down her cheeks. "He is."

He nodded and covered her hand with his. "In any case, I don't want you going to town alone for any reason and if she shows up here, you ring the triangle immediately."

"I will and thank you, Andrew, for everything."

He squeezed her hand. "You're my wife, and I don't intend to lose another wife and child, especially to some crazy woman."

He removed his hand.

She felt bereft, missing his warmth and the comfort his touch brought her.

Now she just prayed that Mildred didn't find her, but in reality, she didn't have much hope of that. If Mildred made it to Golden City, too many people knew her as Andrew's wife and, as far as she knew, she was the only Victoria in town.

CHAPTER SEVEN

January 9, 1871, Golden City, Colorado Territory

Mildred exited the stage with the help of the driver, who said nothing to her. She didn't care. The man was incompetent. The ride had been horrible, as though he purposely hit every bump and hole in the road. She rubbed her backside, sure she'd be bruised.

The stage stopped in front of the Golden West Hotel, probably as good a place as any to stay in this backward town. She picked up her bulging carpetbag and entered the hotel. No one was at the counter so she pounded the button on the bell several times. When no one showed up immediately, she pounded it again.

"I'm coming. I'm coming. Just hold your horses." A small, white-haired woman appeared, hurrying to the counter. "What can I do for you, miss? Would you like a room? Yes, of course you would." She turned the register around to face Mildred. "Please sign right here." She pointed at the next empty line.

Mildred signed her real name. No reason not to.

"Here you are, room number four at the back. It's quieter back there."

"I want one that overlooks the street, preferably on the second or third floor."

The woman raised her eyebrows but quickly grabbed another key from a cubby hole in the wall behind the registration desk. "Oh, well, that would be room eight, second floor on the right at the top of the stairs."

"Thank you," said Mildred and then wondered why she had bothered to thank the woman. She never thanked anyone.

"Here's your key, checkout is at eleven, a bathing room is at the end of the hall and a chamber pot under the bed. If there is anything else you need, let me know. I'm Effie. Effie Washington."

I won't share a bathing room. Hopefully water and a basin are in the room. Mildred took the key without so much as a nod of gratitude. Then she turned back.

"Do you know a Victoria Coleman?"

The woman narrowed her eyes a bit and shook her head. "Can't say as I do."

This time Mildred nodded her thanks. What was the matter with her?

————

Effie watched the rude woman trudge up the stairs and called for Gavin, her grand-nephew.

The young man appeared, wearing an apron and carrying a potato and a paring knife.

————

Victoria was coming down the stairs carrying the laundry basket with dirty clothes inside. Tomorrow was laundry day.

A knock sounded on the door just as she reached the bottom.

The knock sounded again.

"I'm coming. I'm coming." She opened the door and saw Gavin Washington standing on the porch. "Well, Gavin, come in. Is Effie all right?"

The young man took off his hat and held it in his hands in front of him. "Oh, yes, ma'am but she sent me here to see you. A rude, mean and nasty woman, according to Aunt Effie, is looking for you. She wanted me to come to warn you."

Victoria's pulse raced and she dropped the laundry basket. She'd found her. Mildred was here. "Thank you for the information, Gavin. Wait just a moment, I'll write a note to Effie, thanking her, and get you a tip."

He shook his head. "No need for either, Mrs. Mayfield. We try to look after our own, and that includes you." He put on his hat and tipped it. "Good day, ma'am."

"Good day, Gavin, and thank you for coming all the way out here."

"Twernt no trouble. Got me out of peeling spuds." He grinned. "Reckon I'll just mosey on back. Maybe Aunt Effie will be done with the potatoes."

Victoria chuckled. "I'll put a good word in for you with Effie next time I see her. Tell your aunt thank you."

"Yes, ma'am, I will."

She closed the door and picked up the laundry basket.

Andrew came in from the kitchen, removing his gloves and shoving them into the pockets of his sheepskin coat. "Was that young Gavin Washington I saw leaving? What's he doing all the way out here?"

Victoria turned toward him. He must have seen the terror

on her face because he hurried across the floor and wrapped
his arms around her.

"What? What's the matter?"

She pulled back and looked up at him. "She's here.
Mildred. She's here. Effie sent Gavin to tell me that a woman
was looking for me. It's only a matter of time now before she
figures out where I'm at." Stepping away from him, she began
to pace. "Mildred can't be trusted. I believe she'll do whatever
it takes to get to me and if she believes that's through Suse,
she'll use her. Suse can't play in the yard anymore unless we
are out there with her. Just because it's fenced doesn't mean
it's safe. Not anymore."

"It'll be all right."

She nodded and stopped pacing. "Okay. I won't worry
about Suse now all I have to do is worry about Mildred. Can
you teach me how to shoot? Mildred won't hesitate to use a
gun on me. For years she's belonged to a elite club where they
shoot clay pigeons for sport."

"Shoot what?"

"They toss clay disks called pigeons into the air and you
shoot at them with a shotgun. The more you shoot down the
better. She was always boasting that she was a better shot
than David."

His mouth flattened into a thin line. "I have a small gun I
got for Elise to carry in her apron pocket. We had some
trouble with outlaws and Indians when we first got here, so I
taught her to shoot. I probably should have taught you, too.
But that time is passed. We'll go out behind the barn, and I'll
teach you how to shoot it. It's cold outside so bundle up. I'll
get some cans to shoot at."

Victoria got her coat and gloves. She stopped by the
kitchen.

"Nora, Andrew and I are going behind the barn so he can
teach me how to shoot. Keep an eye on Suse. Don't let her go

outside for any reason. A woman from New York is looking to do me harm and may try to use Suse to do so."

"I'll keep track of her. Might be best if she were to play in the kitchen with the puppies. At least I'll know where she's at. What does this woman look like?"

She pulled on her gloves. "She's blonde, blue eyed and pretty. That will work for a while, but she'll get bored because she can't pick them up. You can let her pet them. She hasn't done that before, so that will keep her occupied. And tell her to be sure and pet Daisy, too."

Nora nodded. "Will do. Now, go learn to shoot."

Victoria hugged Nora and went out the back door toward the barn.

The air was frigid. Cold enough she could see her breath as she walked through the barn to the far side. Andrew awaited her.

"Did you get the cans set up?" she asked as she approached.

He pointed to a row of stumps, each with a can on the top.

"It looks like this isn't the first time someone has needed target practice."

"No, I brought Elise back here when I taught her." He pulled a revolver from the belt at his waist. It looked just like his, but smaller. "Today you'll learn the basics...how to load and unload, how to aim and fire, and how to do it calmly. If you get in too much of a hurry, you'll make mistakes and mistakes can get you killed. Understand?"

Killed? Mistakes can get me killed. She swallowed hard and nodded. "I understand, and I'm ready to learn."

He handed her the weapon, handle first.

It felt heavy in her hand, but she supposed that was good rather than it feeling light and insubstantial.

"Now, watch me." He pulled his weapon from his holster.

"Your gun works the same way. First open the cylinder and use the push rod to empty the chambers. Then you can reload the bullets like this." He shoved a cartridge into each empty chamber and clicked the cylinder into place and then holstered his gun.

"Let's see if you can do it with your gun."

She did exactly what he did. The bullets for her gun were smaller than the ones for his.

He grinned. "Wonderful. Now let's see if you can shoot." Turning to face the cans, he pulled his pistol, and fired hitting six out of six.

"That's terrific. You got them all."

He nodded. "I shot slowly, aiming each shot and squeezing the trigger. Nothing hard about it, unless you're under pressure and have to shoot quickly. That will likely put your aim off, and you'll miss the target. Hopefully, you'll still get a part of the person and keep them from shooting you."

She took the gun he'd given her...Elise's gun, aimed it like he did and pulled the trigger.

He chuckled. "You'll do better if you keep your eyes open to see where you're shooting."

"Oh my, did I really close my eyes?"

He nodded. "You did. Try again, only this time keep your eyes open and watch where the bullet goes."

She tried again, and again closed her eyes.

Andrew was as patient a teacher of learning to shoot as he had been in teaching her to make love.

By the time, she was on the sixth can she was thoroughly frustrated with herself. "Why can't I keep my eyes open? I don't understand." She aimed and fired, just wanting to get this over with, and hit the can.

She looked from the can to Andrew, her eyes wide. "I did it. I did it."

He grinned. "You also kept your eyes open."

"I stopped trying to keep them open and just concentrated on aiming and squeezing the trigger."

"Good. Keep it up. Now reload and let's do it again."

She pushed the spent cartridges out with the push rod and reloaded the cylinder before shoving it back into the gun.

Then she fired. Again and again. Repeated the process over and over.

Finally, she let the weapon hang in her hand at her side. "I don't think I can lift this again. My arm is exhausted."

He took the pistol from her. "That's enough. You know what you're doing, and I'm comfortable that you'll be fine should you need to use the weapon to protect yourself and Suse."

"With Mildred in town, I may have to use this sooner rather than later."

He nodded once. "We'll be ready for her."

Then he took her hand in his and together they walked to the house. As they walked through the barn, she stopped at the tack room and got a sugar cube for each of the horses from the box she kept there.

"You'll spoil them," he admonished her, though there was no heat in his words.

"They deserve to be spoiled a little. Someday they'll probably save my life."

"You never know, they just might."

When she finished giving the horses their treats, Andrew took her hand and they walked to the house. Upon walking in the kitchen she was assailed with heavenly aromas.

"Yum, what is that scent, chicken soup? It smells wonderful."

Nora laughed. "You just think that because you've come from the barn. This will be chicken and dumplings. It's one of the men's favorites but I don't make it often because they can eat so many. You need to eat them as they come out of the broth. They can't be kept around staying warm. They'll get gummy."

Victoria walked to the stove and waved her hand over the pot, pushing the scent toward her. "As soon as I get back, you must tell me how to make this. I can see making it for a late night snack, if it's not too hard."

"That'd be great." Andrew licked his lips and rubbed his hands together. "I can't wait."

"Well, you have to wait. I'm not fixing it for a snack when we're having it for dinner tonight."

He frowned and then smiled again. "How about tomorrow night?"

Victoria let out a chortle and then laughed harder. Her husband was teasing her. What did that mean?

She looked up at him. He was smiling and had a mischievous twinkle in his eyes. A twinkle she liked. A lot. Maybe their relationship would survive after all.

CHAPTER EIGHT

Mildred walked around town, stopping in every business she passed, asking about Victoria. No one seemed to know her. She blew out a deep breath. More than likely, she suspected, they were protecting her. Why did everyone want to protect the husband-stealing witch?

After all, it wasn't like Mildred was at fault for the state of her marriage. Or the fact that David never looked at her with affection anymore. Okay, she might be difficult sometimes, and she might complain sometimes, nor did she have the time of day to give to her daughter...or her husband, but she had more important things to do. Like attracting that handsome young man next door to her home.

She straightened her gloves, patted her hat and her hair, and entered the mercantile. A young man stood behind the counter and she hoped she might have better luck with him.

"Hi, there, sir."

He looked up and his eyebrows lifted.

She knew that look. He liked what he saw. She wasn't surprised. After all, she was still a beautiful woman, and she knew it.

"Yes, ma'am, what can I do for you?"

"I'm looking for my dear friend Victoria Coleman. I know she married fairly recently, but for the life of me I can't remember her husband's name."

"Oh, yes ma'am. That would probably be Mrs. Mayfield. She and Andrew haven't been married that long."

She smiled even wider at learning Victoria's new name. Her heart pounded "Yes, that's the name. Can you tell me how to get to her house?"

He chuckled. "Oh, she don't have no house here in town. They live on a ranch about twelve miles outside of town. But if you wait until Saturday, they'll most likely be in for their weekly grocery order."

"What a good idea. Thank you, young man, and if you'd like to get to know me better, I'm at the Golden West Hotel. Mildred Thomas is my name. I'm in room eight on the second floor." She winked at the naïve youngster who had to be at least fifteen years her junior. She wouldn't get any more information, but she just might get a bed-mate for her time here in town. Mildred grinned. Her stay here just got a lot more interesting.

———

After the woman departed, Ed Swanson, the owner of the mercantile, came out from the back room.

"How'd I do, Pa?"

"Real good, son. Real good. Now Andrew can deal with the woman in his own time and won't be surprised by her. Ride on out there, and let him know that the trap, for a lack of a better word, has been laid."

"Yes, sir. I sure hope we did the right thing. I don't care for that woman at all. She's pretty enough, but did you hear her? Like two cats fighting in an alley. I feel sorry for her husband having to hear that every day."

"Yup. Me, too."

The younger man looked after the woman who had smiled wide when she left the counter and then looked at his father. Each of them had an involuntary shudder.

————

When a knock sounded on the front door, Victoria left the kitchen.

She opened the door and when she saw Todd Swanson with his hat in his hands, she smiled.

"Todd, come in. It's much too cold out there to stand on the porch."

He stepped inside.

She closed the door.

"Now, what brings you all this way?"

"Is Andrew around?"

She nodded. "Yes, actually I think he's out at the corral breaking some horses."

"Not anymore. I spotted a rider coming in while I was on my way back." Andrew walked in from the direction of the kitchen. "What can I do for you?" He slapped his hat on his pants.

"My pa sent me to tell you that the trap has been laid."

Andrew perked up. "So soon? Good. I want this matter done and over with."

"Andrew, what matter?" Victoria turned and looked at her husband, lifting her brows, curiosity warring with courtesy. Her pulse began to race. Could this be about Mildred?

"I'll tell you in a moment." He turned back toward Todd. "Give your father my thanks and thank you, too." Andrew extended his hand toward the young man.

"You're welcome. I wish you luck. That woman is a trial. I feel sorry for her husband." Todd shuddered.

"From what I've heard, we should all feel sorry for him." said Andrew. "Ride back to town safely."

"Sure thing." He stepped back and put on his hat then tipped it to Victoria. "Good to see you, ma'am."

"Todd, it's Victoria."

"Yes, ma'am, I mean, Victoria." He grinned. "Old habits are hard to break."

He opened the door and closed it behind him.

"Care to tell me what's going on? I assume you've laid a trap for Mildred."

He nodded. "I've finally let her know where you are. I want to deal with her on my terms and to get the woman's mettle."

"She has no mettle. No honor. Nothing about her is decent, except the man she roped into marrying her."

She knew their situation was similar but refused to be ashamed of what she'd done. Though she was sorry she'd hurt Andrew.

"But David loves Margie more than life itself, even though she's not his child. He'd do anything for that little girl. Her mother ignores her. If she didn't have David, she wouldn't have anyone."

Andrew lifted an eyebrow. "Not too much different from our home."

"I realize that and I'm sorry for it. For my using you. You can still divorce me. I wouldn't blame you if you did. You don't love me." Her heart broke as she tossed out the words. Saying them somehow made it seem worse. "If you're not married to me you might find someone you love."

He walked forward and put his arms around her waist. "Suse loves you. I already told you, I won't take someone away from her again." He leaned down and took her lips with his.

The kiss was sweet and then suddenly it wasn't, and he was demanding. Demanding she respond and she did. She wrapped her arms around his neck and kissed him back, welcoming his tongue when he pressed her lips with his.

She wasn't sure how long they were like that before she felt a tug on her skirt.

Andrew must have had a tug, as well, because he pulled his head back and looked down. "Hi, Suse. What do you need, baby girl?"

"I want kisses, too."

He laughed and stepped back before picking up their daughter. Then he started kissing her all over her face.

She giggled. "Daddy. Daddy, stop."

"But you wanted kisses." Then he started kissing her again.

She giggled and giggled.

Victoria laughed, loving the sound of Suse's giggles. A baby's giggles were contagious and, to her, Suse was still a baby. Her baby.

Andrew finally pulled back and grinned at their daughter. "Enough?"

Suse continued to laugh and nodded. Then she laid her head on Andrew's shoulder. "I wove you, Daddy."

"I love you, too, baby girl."

Victoria saw the tears in his eyes, but he held them in. She felt hot tears stinging her own eyes.

"I wove you, too, Toria."

"Ah, Suse, I love you, too."

This was such a precious moment, with a lump in her throat, Victoria knew she would remember it forever.

Suse began to squirm. "Down now."

"What do you say?" asked Victoria.

"Pease."

"Good girl," said Andrew and put her on the floor.

She ran off toward the kitchen, sure to beg a cookie from Nora before lunch.

Victoria watched her go and wiped at her eyes. "She is the sweetest little thing." She turned to Andrew. "You know I love her, don't you? That I would give my life for her?"

He ran a knuckle down her cheek. "I suspected. She's hard not to love."

Just like her father. "So, tell me more about this trap. What can I do to help you?"

"Come into my office."

She followed him down the hall toward the kitchen, turning at the first door on the right.

"Please close the door behind you and sit."

She complied and then turned toward him. "Now, what did he mean?"

Andrew began to pace behind her, where she sat in front of his desk. Directly behind the desk was a window looking out on the rest of the ranch. On either side of the window along that long wall were bookshelves.

"I've been working with some of the local businesses to deal with Mildred on my terms. They let it slip who you are married to. It won't take her long to figure out where we live. I want to get Mildred where she's a known entity."

"Isn't that kind of like inviting the fox into the hen house?" *Mildred is sneaky, I'd feel a lot better if she didn't know where I live.*

He chuckled. "Yes, I guess it is, but sometimes the only way to deal with the fox is inside the hen house."

She fidgeted in her chair. "I guess I don't understand."

"I want her to see what she's up against. I want her to understand that if she ever returns to my land, I'll shoot her as a trespasser. I want her to see you, but I don't want her to know you are armed. You are armed, aren't you?"

She cocked her head. "What do you think? I've got my weapon in my apron pocket." I need to find another way to carry it. Suse is the perfect size to bump it or grab it. I don't want an accident to happen."

"That's true. I'll make you a holster. To heck if she sees you're armed. Maybe that will be a good thing. Besides, she'll see all the men and they will all have their weapons drawn or holding their rifles. I want her to know I protect what's mine, and you're mine."

Victoria looked down at her lap. She loved hearing those words and hoped more than just possession was behind them. She hoped that, maybe, the words were the beginning of his falling in love with her. Hope was all she had right now, and she kept it close to her heart.

———

The next day, Victoria was dusting in the parlor when she heard Daisy bark. She went to the parlor window and watched as a buggy came to a stop in front of the house.

Mildred tethered the reins to the brake and climbed down. She checked a small derringer and returned it to her bag.

Victoria patted her own gun.

Mildred walked up the path to the porch and then to the front door where she knocked.

Removing her pistol from her pocket, she opened the front door. To heck with keeping it hidden. She wanted Mildred to know she wouldn't go easily.

She opened the door and kept her gun behind her. "Mildred. What brings you all this way?"

"Why you, Victoria." She reached in her bag and removed her derringer.

"If you shoot her, you'll die where you stand."

Mildred gasped and dropped her gun and swung toward him. "Who are you?"

He walked up the porch from the side yard. "I'm Andrew Mayfield, Victoria's husband, and I had you come here for a specific purpose. I want you to see Victoria and know she means the world to me. I protect what's mine, Mrs. Thomas. If you set foot on this land again, I'll have you shot for trespassing and no court will charge me." He stopped in front of her. "Understand?"

Mildred looked at them. "Yes. I understand." She reached for the gun she dropped.

"You can leave that. You won't need it. If I were you, I'd be on the next stage back to Denver, and then the train back to New York."

Eyes narrowed, she backed away from Andrew. "That would seem the prudent thing to do." She turned toward the buggy and gasped again.

All the men from Ben to Zach were in the yard, weapons drawn.

Andrew's arm spread wide, taking in all the men. "They have orders to shoot you on sight, so don't think it's just me you have to watch out for. I know you thought you could get around me, but do you really think you can get around all ten of them?"

She shook her head. "No. I know when I'm defeated...for the moment." She pointed toward Victoria's belly. "But I will see that little bastard dead. No one will challenge Margery's claim on David's assets."

Victoria placed her hands over her belly. "David is not the father of my child. When will you get that simple fact through your head? This child is mine." She looked up at Andrew. "Ours."

"What's ours?" asked Suse, as she hurried down the stairs, one step at a time.

Victoria turned away from Mildred, placed her gun back in her pocket and squatted down in front of the child. "Our baby. You'll have a new baby sister or brother. Would you like that?"

Suse nodded fast. "Yup. Then we can pay wif the puppies." She turned and ran toward the kitchen.

Mildred narrowed her eyes and cocked a brow. "So you have a child. That's very interesting."

Andrew stepped in front of Mildred until he was just inches from her. "If you touch my daughter, I'll kill you... wherever you are."

Mildred raised an eyebrow and lifted her chin. "Okay, I was just commenting. That's all."

"I know what you were doing. Just remember what I said. Now, get off my land."

Mildred lifted her skirt and ran back to the buggy, climbed in and whipped the horses into a gallop.

They watched her go.

Andrew put an arm around Victoria's shoulders. Then he called to his crew. "Thanks, men. She'll be back but likely not today. Go on back to work but remain vigilant."

The men dispersed and disappeared behind the house.

She leaned into him. Her nerves were fried and she felt like she'd been doing laundry all day. Her body hurt from the tension. "Did you see the way she looked at Suse? We can't ever leave her alone. I'm sure Mildred will be back. She'll just be sneakier about it. She knows how to ride a horse so the next time, she won't bring the buggy."

He nodded. "I saw the way she looked at my baby. I

meant what I said. I will see her dead if she touches so much as a strand of Suse's hair."

"So will I."

He squeezed her shoulders. "I know you will. I have to go back to work, but I'd been watching for her to show up, doing chores around the outside of the house that I'd been putting off. I was sure it would be today, since Todd came out yesterday."

"I'm surprised she waited until today. I expect her to try again this week, but I think she'll let things die down for a couple of days."

"Me, too, but we'll remain vigilant."

Victoria pulled away, walked inside and into the kitchen.

Andrew followed her and closed the door behind him.

"Do you have time for coffee?"

"I'd love to, but I really need to get to work."

She grinned. "So do I, but I don't want to."

Suse suddenly squealed. She was behind the stove with the puppies.

"She bit me. Sally bit me."

Victoria held out her arms. "Come here, let me see."

The puppies had their milk teeth, sharp little things.

"There's barely a scratch. Why did the puppy bite you?"

Suse put her right index finger in her mouth and looked down.

"Suse? What were you doing that you shouldn't have?" asked Andrew.

She started to cry. "I just want to hold her."

"She was nursing, wasn't she?" asked Victoria.

"Uh huh."

Andrew crossed his arms over his chest. "What have we told you about picking up the puppies?"

"Not to pick up puppies."

Andrew seemed to ignore her tears. "And why are you not to pick them up?"

"They too little. Need to get bigger."

Victoria looked in the box to make sure Sally had found her mama again. The poor puppy was on its back and kicking. She picked her up and put her back with her mama. "That's right. Sally was just looking for her mama's teat so she could eat and you took that away from her. Do you like it when you don't get to eat your dinner?"

Suse shook her head.

Victoria stood. "Now, you can no longer be near the puppies unless your Daddy or I are with you. So that won't be very often. We both have chores to do and can't be spending the day with you at the puppies. Understand?"

Suse looked down and swayed back and forth. "Uh huh. I sorry. Didn't mean to hurt Sally."

Andrew shook his head. "But you did. You dropped her and left her on her back. She was scared, and you didn't take care of her. That's not good. Now, go to your room. You can play up there until lunch time."

Suse began to cry in earnest and started to scream and stamp her feet.

Victoria took her hand and headed out of the kitchen.

Suse dropped to the floor and refused to walk.

"That's enough, young lady." Andrew scooped her into his arms and carried her to her room.

Victoria let them go. Though she loved Suse, when Andrew was in the same room, he should be the one to mete out discipline.

He returned shortly.

"How is she?"

"Crying and laying on the floor. I shut the door to her room and told her if I caught her out of it, I'd spank her little bottom."

Victoria lifted her brows and widened her eyes. "You wouldn't really spank her, would you?"

"I'd have to. You have to follow through with your promises or she won't ever believe you and will do as she wishes. I won't hurt anything but her pride. Just a swat. But she'll know that I mean what I say."

She nodded. *The nuns delivered much more severe discipline when I was in the orphanage. They used their rulers, or paddles, to spank the children who misbehaved. I only got whipped once. That was enough. I learned never to disobey again.* "Yes, you're right. She has to learn to mind."

"Exactly. Now I'm off to finish breaking a few horses. I'll be back for dinner." Then he gave her a kiss on the cheek and walked out of the kitchen.

Victoria placed her fingers on her cheek, still burning from the touch of his lips and decided feelings for her were definitely there. But were those feelings love?

CHAPTER NINE

Mildred whipped the horses into a gallop and kept them there most of the way to town. When the animals started to have difficulty, she finally slowed down.

What's the matter with me? I know better than to treat horses this way. Killing the animals and getting stuck out on the prairie in the middle of nowhere wouldn't do me any good.

Interesting. A little girl who looked just like Margery. Victoria has probably already fallen in love with her. I can use that when I go back. I don't believe for a moment that Mayfield will kill me. I know his type...he's too honorable, just like David. And, just like David, I know how to manipulate him to my ends. All I need is that little girl of his, and he'll give me Victoria. He'll do anything for that child. I saw the love in his eyes, though he tried to hide it. Yes, the child is the key.

———

Saturday, February 4, 1871

. . .

The puppies were a month old now and were eager to be out of the box. Luckily, they couldn't get out on their own. Victoria let them run around the kitchen once each day so they could stretch their little legs.

Andrew sat at the table with a cup of coffee and the Golden Transcript newspaper, a couple of puppies chewing on his boots.

Victoria was gathering the puppies to put them back in the box and bent over to get the two by his feet.

"You know, we need a bigger place for the puppies. The box is just too small."

He looked up and laid his paper on the table. "It's time for them to go to the barn with the cats."

Alarmed, she widened her eyes. "We can't do that. Daisy is used to being in the house, not the barn."

Andrew put up his hands and shook his head once. "Well, what would you have me do?"

"Well." She held a puppy in each hand. "I was thinking we could take the table out of the dining room and put them in there. I don't want them to chew the table legs and I don't want to have to get under the table to clean up their messes. We don't use the room, anyway. You can just take the table apart and set it against the wall or move it to the storage shed or the barn."

He rubbed his chin.

He looked as though he was pulling a beard to a point.

"That could work and you can train them to go outside. In the meantime, you'll have to cover the floor with news-paper to protect it."

"Yes, I know."

"Are you sure you want to take that job on in your condi-tion? You're five months pregnant now and with each passing day it will be harder for you to deal with the little dogs."

"It's only for a month or less. Daisy is already beginning to wean them, and I've started feeding them bits of leftover meat cut very small. You should see them chow down on that."

He chuckled. "I bet they do. I hope you give some to Daisy, too."

"Of course, I do." Victoria tried to put her hands on her hips but remembered she held the pups. She turned and put them in the box with their mother and the rest of their siblings. Then she returned to the table and stood by him.

"So what do you think of my idea, and can you do it today?"

He sat back in his chair and laughed. "So you know, I'll say yes even though you just asked?"

She nodded. "You want to please me and this will, so you'll do it for me."

He grabbed her around the waist and pulled her onto his lap.

She squealed. "Andrew!"

"Now, ask me nicely."

She grinned. He was being playful, and she liked it. "Please, take down the table in the dining room for the puppies." She wrapped her arms around his neck and kissed his chin. "Pretty please?" She kissed his cheeks. "Pretty, pretty please?" She fitted her lips to his and kissed him, running her tongue along his closed lips.

He smiled and opened his mouth, meeting her tongue with his.

She tasted him, the coffee he drank, and a touch of his minty tooth powder.

"Daddy, you eat Toria?"

Andrew choked and then laughed.

Victoria felt the heat in her cheeks, but she chuckled.

"No, baby girl, I'm just kissing Victoria."

"Why you do that all time?"

"Because I like kissing Victoria."

"I kiss Toria, too. I kiss you, too."

Andrew lifted Suse onto his lap. "Now I'm holding both my girls." He kissed Suse's cheek and Victoria kissed her other cheek.

Victoria moved to get up. "Well, this girl needs to get up and do her chores."

Andrew released her. "I suppose that means I need to do my chores, too. I have to green break horses for the army today, hence my sitting here reading the paper."

"Why don't you have the men break the horses?"

"Because I do it faster and better than they do. They can do the job, but not as well."

"Perhaps they need more practice. They won't get that as long as you keep doing the job."

He shrugged. "I suppose I like it, too. It's exciting."

She studied her husband, as he kissed his daughter again before putting her on the floor.

"You go upstairs and play now, Suse," said Victoria.

"I play with puppies." She gazed up at Victoria. "Pease, Toria. Pease."

Victoria put her hands on her hips. "You can play with one puppy. I don't want all of them out of the box, I just got them put back in there. Tell me which one you want to play with."

"I play with Patches. I haven't played with him yet."

Suse sat on the floor in the middle of the kitchen. That was where Victoria had her sit anytime she played with the pups.

Victoria picked up Patches and set the puppy on the floor about two feet from Suse. This was her habit to see if any of them went to her—picked her out. As soon as she set Patches down, he yipped and ran to Suse.

"Toria you see that? Patches come to me."

"That's wonderful. He chose you. Have you decided what puppy you want to keep?"

"I think I keep Patches 'cause'n he likes me, too."

"I think he's a wonderful choice."

Victoria looked up at Andrew.

He smiled.

Victoria pointed at Suse. "Did you see? He didn't go back to the box or go exploring, he went right to her."

Andrew put his thumbs in his pockets. "I saw."

Victoria turned back to Suse. "He's a good puppy. Look how happy he is. His whole bottom is wagging, not just his tail. Oh, Andrew, you have to make the dining room a puppy room now, so Suse can bond with Patches even more."

He crossed his arms over his chest. "I can see I won't have any rest until I get that done, so breaking the horses will have to wait. I'll go get a couple of the boys to help me with the project. It's definitely at least a three, maybe four extra men job. I can't lift that tabletop by myself. It's solid wood and about ten feet long."

"You must have help. Ben, Ray and Zach are the biggest men. If they can help you, you'll have it done in nothing flat."

He got his coat from a peg on the wall. "All right, I'm going. We'll be right back." He walked out the back door.

Victoria grinned and clasped her hands together, stretching her arms down in front of her. Her plan was coming together and the puppies would no longer be under foot. They'd be able to run around, stretch their legs and get strong. Suse could go in and play with them.

Victoria knew she'd have to clean up after them daily and she would have to teach them to go outside or at least on a specific paper in the corner, but she could do it. One puppy at a time.

Too bad, it wouldn't be as easy to get Andrew to love her. She didn't know what else she could do. She was as loving toward him as she could be and still he wouldn't tell her he loved her. He was kind and gentle with her. He took her opinions into account before making a decision that would affect her. Was that love?

She didn't really know, but she suspected that maybe he was in love with her and just wouldn't admit it, to himself or to her.

————

It was time. She hadn't returned to the Mayfield ranch for a month. Long enough for them to let down their guard. She rode to the ranch, sticking to the forest that the ranch butted up against. She watched and waited. If she had to, she'd come back every day until she saw the situation she wanted.

It appeared she wouldn't have to wait, after all. The little girl came out of the house carrying something...a puppy. She put down the puppy and started to play with it.

Mildred watched for about five minutes and saw no one else come out. The time was now or never to take the child. She rode into the ranch yard and called the child.

"Hello. My name is Mildred. I'm a friend of Victoria's. Would you like a candy stick?"

"Uh huh." The child toddled over to Mildred who gave her the candy stick and then picked her up and over the picket fence.

The child began to cry.

"Hush now. Victoria will come for you soon enough." Mildred dropped a note in the yard and put the little girl on the horse, climbing up behind her. Mildred put the child on her lap and galloped away.

————

"Suse. Suse, where are you?" Could she have gone outside? She knew she wasn't supposed to go outside. But she was only three and probably forgot. Victoria knew their memories were short.

She ran out the front door.

Patches greeted her at the bottom of the steps, yipping wildly.

"Oh, my God." She noticed a piece of paper fluttering by the fence and hurried to pick it up.

Victoria,

If you want to see the child alive again, you'll come to me, alone. The Golden West Hotel, room eight.

Mildred

Victoria fell to her knees. A keening wail emanated from her. She stood and ran inside and to the kitchen. She went out the back door and rang the triangle.

Andrew was the first to show up.

All the men came from their jobs.

Victoria took Andrew by the sides of his coat. "She's gone. Mildred has her. Suse. Mildred has Suse."

He frowned. "How? She was supposed to be in here with you."

She closed her eyes for a moment and willed the tears away. "I thought she was in with the puppies, but she took Patches and went outside. I didn't know. I didn't hear anything. I went to check on her in the puppy room and found her missing, so I went outside and found this note."

He quickly read the note. "You can't go there alone. This woman means to kill you."

"If I don't go, she will kill Suse. She has nothing to lose now since she's kidnapped her. You need to go to the sheriff and tell him what has happened."

"I will. After you get Suse out of the room and I have her, then Samuel and I will come and arrest Mildred."

"Hopefully, before she does anything to me. I'll put Suse outside the room and tell her to go down to Effie."

He grabbed her by her upper arms. "No. I can't let you go."

She closed her eyes and tilted her head. Then she opened them again and looked into his worried gaze. "You have no choice. I have no choice. I won't let anything happen to Suse." She could tell Andrew was torn. She placed a hand on his arm. "It's the only way, Andrew. The only way we can assure Suse's safety."

He pulled her into his arms. "I don't want to lose you."

She leaned back and looked into his beloved face. "You won't lose me. I won't let her kill me without a fight." She placed a hand on her rounded stomach. "I have too much to live for. You must make sure she's safe." *You have to do what I didn't. You have to keep our baby girl safe above all else.*

"I'll wait until Suse is safely away and then I'll come for you."

She smiled. "I'd appreciate it."

He didn't smile back but took her in his arms and held her close. "I won't let her take you from me and Suse."

"You might bring Doc with you, just in case."

"I'll come in the back of the building so she can't see me come in. Room eight looks out over the street, so I'll have to go behind the businesses to come in unnoticed."

"Please be careful. Mildred is desperate, but she's not stupid. At least not too stupid."

"I suppose so. Shall we go? I want to get Suse back as soon as possible. Once we get to town, I'll ride and you take the buggy."

"Yes, that's best. Once she sees that I'm the only one in the buggy, she'll relax some. Will you bring the men with you? As backup?"

"No, I'll be bringing Samuel. And hopefully she won't be looking for anyone else, when she sees only you."

She gave him a kiss. "Let's go get our daughter back."

He smiled and nodded. "I'll bring the buggy up here with my horse tied to the back."

"Okay. Mildred is not good with children and I fear what she'll do if Suse throws a temper tantrum."

Andrew frowned. "She hurts my...our...daughter, and I'll see her dead."

"Yes, we will. But neither of us will kill her. You'll have Samuel arrest her. That's his job. I don't want either of us in prison or hung for murder, though she may deserve it. They may hang her anyway. Kidnapping is a crime punishable by death in many jurisdictions."

"All right, cooler heads will prevail."

———

They arrived at the curve in the road before it went into the town. Andrew pulled the buggy to a stop and handed the reins to Victoria. "I'll untie my horse and meet you in the hotel." He leaned over and kissed her.

"Don't be too long."

"I won't."

Victoria set the horses to a trot and went directly down the middle of Main Street. The Golden West Hotel was at the end of the street facing her. As she got closer, her anger flared. *How dare this woman try to take my family from me? How dare she threaten to kill me just so she can also kill my baby?*

She turned the horses, so they were parallel to the hotel and climbed down. Then she ran up the steps to the porch and into the lobby.

Effie Washington was waiting for her sitting on a chair in front of the registration desk.

"Victoria. I know she's got Suse, but there was nothing I could do without harming the child. I did send Todd to get Samuel. I don't know where he is."

"Don't worry Effie. That's why I'm here. Would you go get Doc? I fear someone will need his services before all is said and done."

"Sure thing." The little, white-haired lady hurried out of the hotel and turned right.

Victoria girded herself for what was to come. She'd brought her gun and she might have the advantage since Andrew had confiscated Mildred's derringer. She doubted Mildred would let her keep it or allow her to use it, but she might get a chance.

CHAPTER TEN

She hurried up the stairs to room eight, stopped outside and knocked on the door. "Mildred, I'm here. Let me in." Victoria searched the hallway for something...anything...she could use for a weapon, but found none. She heard Suse screaming.

"Ow. Dat hurts. Toria! Toria, help!"

Victoria's heart broke hearing her sweet daughter's distress.

Mildred answered the door. She had Suse by her ponytail not letting her go and she had a gun aimed at Suse.

She must have bought another weapon or had two derringers with her.

"I knew you'd come. The brat looks like my Margery and I know how you loved her. Come in, Victoria."

"Let Suse go."

Mildred narrowed her eyes.

For a moment fear burned a hole into Victoria. Fear she wouldn't let her daughter go. She held her breath for a moment.

"Fine. She's been nothing but a pain in my backside since I took her. Calling for you, for Patches, and her Daddy." She gave Suse a shove. "Go. Get. Get out of here before I change my mind."

Suse grabbed Victoria's skirts. "Toria." She sniffled.

Victoria's heart started beating again and she knelt. "Suse, I want you to listen to me. You go straight down those stairs and go see Aunt Effie, okay?"

Suse nodded.

"I'll be right down. But you go on ahead."

The child ran to the stairs and went down them slowly one at a time holding on to the uprights.

When Victoria could no longer see her, she went into the room with Mildred.

Mildred backed away from the door, keeping her gun on Victoria. "She's not your daughter. You didn't have to come. I doubt I would have killed her."

She kept her demeanor calm, holding her hands to her sides. "But I don't know that do I? I'm not sure you do either. You've gotten quite bloodthirsty, Mildred."

"Perhaps. But first put that gun of yours on the floor and kick it to me."

Victoria took the gun out of her apron pocket, set it on the carpet and kicked it at Mildred as hard as she could, hoping it would hurt her or surprise her enough she'd drop her weapon.

She didn't. Instead, the weapon was stopped by her skirt.

"Nice try, Victoria. Nice try, but it will take more than that to make me drop this gun."

Disappointed Victoria looked around for anything else she could use as a weapon and found none. Now, she wondered how long she'd have to stall before Andrew could save her.

———

Suse finally appeared on the stairs and Effie went to her.

Andrew didn't realize he'd been holding his breath until he saw Suse and started breathing again. He didn't want Suse to see him because she would likely yell his name across the lobby. Mildred might hear and shoot Victoria. He couldn't risk that, so he stayed out of sight.

Effie spoke to the child. "Suse are you all right? Do you want some cookies and milk? I've got some in the kitchen. Come with me." The old woman took the child's hand, and they walked together to the kitchen. Effie chattered and kept Suse's mind off of what was happening.

Andrew watched them go and when he was certain that Suse was safe, he bounded quietly up the stairs two at a time. Just as he reached the door a shot rang out. Fearing the worst, he kicked the door in, gun drawn.

The sight that greeted him made his blood run cold. Victoria was on the floor and Mildred stood over her with the gun pointed at her head.

Andrew fired.

Wide-eyed, her mouth shaped in an O, Mildred looked at him and dropped the gun while grabbing her arm with her other hand. "You shot me. You shot me."

"You're lucky the sheriff is with me." He looked down at Victoria who lay on her stomach. He saw a wound on her back where a bullet may have come out. He dropped to his knees and then gazed up at Mildred. "If she dies, I'll finish the job. Samuel!"

Sheriff Banks rushed in and put handcuffs on Mildred, ignoring her wound.

Doc ran in behind the sheriff and knelt beside Victoria. He probed the wound on the back shoulder of her dress with his fingers and then gently turned her over.

She had her hands covering her stomach.

As doc moved her, she began to thrash. "No. Not my baby. No."

"Andrew, pick her up and carry her to my office where I can make sure no fragments of the bullet are in the wound and get her sewed up."

"What about the baby, Doc?" The lump in his throat made it difficult to talk.

Doc reached in his bag and pulled out his stethoscope. He gently moved her hands and listened to her stomach.

"The baby appears to be just fine. Nice strong heartbeat. Now let's get her to the office."

Andrew stepped forward and picked up his wife, the woman who had become more precious to him than gold. He only hoped she could love him back. He hadn't been very good to her. He never told her how he felt. Worse, he let her believe he couldn't love her. Yes, he still loved Elise in a corner of his heart. She was his first real love, but his love for Victoria was a mature, all-consuming kind of love. She filled his heart and healed it.

"Will she be all right, Doc?"

"I believe so, but I need to examine her and make sure I'm not missing anything."

Samuel Banks stood by the window with Mildred. "I have her weapon, and though it fires more than one round, she only fired one. If you don't find any fragments, there won't be any other wounds."

Andrew's heart soared. She would be all right. He would see to it. He'd care for her himself and have one of the cowboys do his chores so he could stay with Victoria.

He carried her downstairs and then two doors up and to the east side of the street to Doc's office.

"This way. Follow me." Doc led the way to the room at the end of a long hall with two doors on either side. "Lay her on that table and remove her clothes. I need to examine her thoroughly."

Andrew set about taking off her dress, then her chemise and bloomers. When she was naked, he stepped back.

Doc brought a sheet and covered her with it. "You don't have to stay, Andrew."

He shook his head. "I'm not going anywhere."

Doc chuckled. "Finally fell in love with your wife, huh? Took long enough."

Andrew felt his ears heat. "I'm a slow learner." He had no other excuse...at least, for Doc. How could he tell him he'd been in love with her for some time, but refused to believe it or admit it? How could he admit to Doc what a fool he'd been? Admitting his love for her would be hard enough.

Doc thoroughly examined Victoria. "There is only the one wound. Now I have to probe it. I don't want her moving, so I'm glad she's unconscious, but she still may feel pain. I need you to hold her down for me without covering the wound."

Andrew placed a hand on to her unwounded shoulder and one on her upper arm on the other side.

Doc probed the injury with his finger and then with an instrument. "I don't feel a thing. I think we're safe to sew her up. I need to clean the wound and that will hurt, a lot, so continue holding her."

He cleaned the outside of the wound on her front and her back and then poured whiskey into the opening.

Victoria screamed and tried to sit up before collapsing onto the table again.

Andrew's heart hurt for his little wife. He hated to see her in so much pain.

Doc quickly sewed up the front, then the back and then wrapped a bandage around her ribcage and over her shoulder, covering the wound.

"You can dress her again now, Andrew. Do you need help?"

"I don't know. I've never done it this way." Now that he knew she would be well, he was able to joke.

Even doc chuckled.

Together, they got her dressed.

"You have the buggy here?"

He nodded. "Yes, and I need to get Suse. She's safe with Effie, having milk and cookies. She probably won't want any dinner. May I leave Victoria here for a moment?"

"I'll watch her and make sure the wound isn't bleeding overly much."

"Thanks, Doc. What do I owe you?" He held out his hand.

Doc shook his hand. "Don't worry about that now. Get your family. I'll send you a bill."

"Thanks." Andrew hurried from the room. He ran over to the hotel and through it to the kitchen.

"Daddy!" Suse slipped off her chair and ran to him. "Where's Mama?"

He smiled. "Mama?"

She ducked her head. "Think Toria let me call her Mama?"

"Oh, baby girl, I think she'll be thrilled. I'm happy, too. I'm so proud of you for being a big girl with the bad lady. You did very well."

Suse hugged him tighter. "Bad lady's gone?"

He hugged her tighter. "Yes, the bad lady is gone. She can't hurt any of us anymore."

———

Two months later, May 5, 1871, Golden, Colorado, Courthouse

Trial of Mildred Thomas

. . .

The prosecutor, Gerald Mason, a man in his late thirties with blonde hair parted in the middle and slicked down, approached the witness chair where David Thomas sat.

"Mr. Thomas, why did your wife leave New York and come to Golden City?"

"She was obsessed with Miss Coleman...er...Mrs. Mayfield's unborn child believing it to be mine. It is not."

"And when she left New York, what did you do?"

"I wired Mrs. Mayfield that Mildred had left and was probably heading her way and to be careful."

"I have no more questions for this witness," said the prosecutor.

Mildred refused an attorney so the judge spoke to her directly. "Mrs. Thomas, do you have any questions for this witness?"

Mildred remained stoic and said nothing.

The judged sighed. "Very well, you may call your next witness, Mr. Mason."

"The prosecution calls Mrs. Victoria Mayfield."

Victoria walked up to the bench and the bailiff swore her in.

Mr. Mason approached her. "Mrs. Mayfield would you tell us what led to your injury?"

"Mrs. Thomas had kidnapped my daughter and left a note for me to come and get her, alone, or she would kill Susannah."

"And did you go alone?"

"In a manner of speaking. I went to her room in the hotel alone, but my husband was downstairs waiting until Susannah came down safely before he came up. After I got Susannah out of the room and headed down the stairs I turned to Mildred. I asked her what now? She responded that now she would kill me that no one would threaten Margery's inheritance. Then she shot me. I moved to protect my child and that is probably the reason I'm alive today."

The judge, who had gray hair and was balding, looked down at Mildred. "Mildred Thomas, do you have anything to say for on your behalf or witnesses you'd like to call?"

Mildred stood. "Nothing, except I wish I hadn't missed."

The crowd began yelling.

"Hang her."

"She's guilty."

The judge pounded his gavel on the desk. "Order. I will have order in the court or I will clear the room."

The crowd settled down.

David Thomas sat with Victoria and Andrew behind the prosecutor.

Again the judge pounded the gavel. "Mildred Thomas, I find you guilty of kidnapping and attempted murder. Your lack of remorse forces me to sentence you to hang by your neck until dead. The sentence is to be carried out tomorrow morning at dawn."

The sentence was carried out, and her body buried in the part of the graveyard for criminals, in an unmarked grave.

CHAPTER ELEVEN

Two weeks later

Victoria was over eight months pregnant now.

Andrew rubbed her belly as they lay in bed. "I'll do your chores from now on."

She covered his hand with hers. "You will do no such thing. I'm still capable of doing my chores and until I can't I'll keep doing them. Remaining active is good for me. Doc says it makes the delivery easier."

Andrew chuckled. "You are a stubborn one, my love."

"I will never tire of hearing you say that."

He pushed up onto his elbow and smiled down at her. "That you're stubborn? I can assure you, I will remind you daily, if you wish."

She swatted him. "Not that. My love. You can call me your love anytime. I love you, too. I've loved you since I first saw you with Suse. You were so loving with her. You were always loving toward me, even when you told me you couldn't ever love me." She searched her thoughts for the right words.

"I tried to tell myself that you just didn't realize your feelings."

He stopped her with two fingers on her lips. "I was a fool. Have you forgiven me yet?"

She kissed his fingers. Happiness filled her that their relationship had grown to this point, where they could just be together and love one another.

He pulled his fingers away and replaced them with his lips. "I love you. More than I ever thought possible. You are mine, Victoria Mayfield." He looked down at her swollen stomach and then ran his hand over it. "And this little one is mine. We will never speak of how he was conceived. It doesn't matter. He is, or she is, my child and I already love him or her."

Victoria's eyes teared, and the moisture traveled down her cheek despite her attempts to stop it.

Andrew took her in his arms. "Here, now. Don't cry."

"I can't help it. I'm tearier since I became pregnant, but we need to get up. The girls will be rising, if they haven't already, and so will David."

Andrew gave her a kiss and rolled out of bed before turning and helping her.

"I can't believe how hard it is to move around with this belly." She sat up and scooted to the side of the bed where she gave him her hand.

He tugged, and she stood.

She put on her bloomers and a chemise. With the top three buttons undone, she pulled her dress over her head. Then she bent over so she could see her shoes and slipped them on.

"Andrew, would you tie my shoes for me, please."

"Of course, my love."

She looked at him as he tied her shoes. "You're being very loving this morning."

"I had a nightmare last night where I'd lost you without ever telling you how I feel. I won't make that mistake again. I intend to tell you *I love you*, everyday."

She cupped his face. His overnight stubble tickled her palm. "I love you, too. For always."

He stood and helped her to her feet. Then he leaned down and kissed her upturned face. He was more than a head taller so he always bent his neck to kiss her and he never seemed to mind.

She pulled away, kissing his cheek. "I must milk the cows so Nora has time to strain the milk. Then I need to gather the eggs for breakfast."

"I'll milk the cow. I can only imagine what moves you have to do to get close enough to milk her."

She chuckled. "I sort of let my stomach hang between my splayed knees."

He rolled his eyes. "You should have let me know long before now. I will take care of the cows from now on. Can you gather the eggs without undue contortions?"

She cocked her head and put her hands on her hips. "Yes, I can gather the eggs. Shall we go?"

He swung his arm wide. "After you, my love."

She walked out of the room, wearing a big smile. In the kitchen she donned her coat, picked up the egg basket and headed out into the cold.

She and Andrew finished with the chores and Nora prepared breakfast.

———

Two little girls, one three and one four, both blonde, one blue eyed, and one with eyes of emerald green, thundered down the stairs.

"Ladies, you will not run in the house," Victoria admonished them.

"Yes, Mama," said Suse.

"Yes, Victoria," said Margie.

They turned to each other and grinned. Then they skipped to the table.

Victoria shook her head and raised her eyes heavenward.

After everyone was seated for breakfast, David cleared his throat.

"I have an announcement to make."

"Go ahead," said Andrew.

"I'm selling my home in New York and moving to Golden City permanently."

Victoria clapped her hands. "Oh, David. That's wonderful. What do you intend to do for a living?"

"The same thing I do now. I'll open a bank and manage my investments. I can handle the investments by wire since they require very little manipulating. I intend to buy a ranch and raise some cattle. I must sell the house in New York and maybe some investments, but I want to buy the ranch outright and not have a note of any kind."

Andrew sat up straight. "I might know of a place near here. The owner is ill and moving to Texas. He hopes the warm weather will help him."

"That would be wonderful. Do you suppose we can look at it today? I'd like to get the ball rolling as soon as possible."

"Sure, we'll go after breakfast."

"I'd love it if you and Margie lived close. I hope it all works out."

———

Andrew and David returned just as the cowboys and the rest of the family were sitting down to eat lunch.

Victoria stood. "Let me get your place settings. Sit, and tell us what you think of the Ledbetter place." She bustled around setting their plates and silverware in front of them.

When they were settled she sat again. "Tell us will you buy the ranch?"

David grinned and nodded. "I already made Mr. Ledbetter an offer, and he accepted. Andrew said I'm getting a good deal."

"He's getting a great deal. The price includes the ranch buildings, house, one-thousand acres of land and two hundred head of cattle. I think the ranch hands will stay and the foreman, Mac Taylor, is willing to teach David the ropes. David couldn't have decided to stay here and buy land at a better time. Old Frank Ledbetter is ready to join his daughter and son-in-law in the Texas hill country in a little town called Kerrville."

"He said I can move-in in about a month, so you'll have me underfoot until after the baby comes. Hope you don't mind."

Victoria, her mouth in a straight line, said, "I'm sorry David. You must find a hotel room."

David's eyebrows rose.

She laughed. "Of course, you can stay. I'm just teasing you." She kept the smile on her face as a contraction hit her making her want to rub her back to ease the pain, but she knew if she did that Andrew would put her in bed and she wasn't ready for that.

Visibly relaxing, David let out a long breath.

Andrew chuckled. "She's been practicing her teasing techniques. She's getting rather good at keeping a straight face."

David nodded. "She had me convinced."

The cowboys around the table shook their heads and chuckled or rolled their eyes. Some of them did all three.

"Victoria," said Ray, a man with nice golden brown hair

and steady blue eyes. "You shouldn't tease your friend. One of these days they'll think you're teasing when you aren't."

She frowned and hung her head. "You're probably right. I'll try to control myself."

Victoria got up to collect the coffee pot and stopped cold in the middle of the kitchen. She turned around. "Andrew, I believe my water just broke. I think I'm having the baby now."

Andrew stood so fast his chair fell over. He hurried to her side and swept her into his arms. "One of you men ride to town and get Doc. Tell him we're having a baby."

"I'll go," said Keet. "I've got the fastest horse." He lit out of the kitchen like his tail was on fire.

Nora stood and got a towel. "I'll be up with hot water and extra towels after I clean up this mess."

"Thank you, Nora," said Victoria.

Andrew headed upstairs.

"Don't worry about the girls, I'll keep them busy," said David.

She couldn't see him, but she heard him.

"Girls, let's go into your room and play until after Victoria has the baby."

"When will that be, Daddy?" asked Margie.

"I don't know. It might be a long time," said David.

Andrew carried her into their bedroom and set her down.

"You know, I'm not having the baby right now. Let's get the oil cloth down on the bed. It's in the closet."

She stripped the bed.

He laid the oil cloth on the mattress.

She covered it with the sheet tucking in the hems.

Then she unbuttoned her dress and hung it on a peg on the wall. She undressed and put on a nightgown. Afterward, she lay on the bed.

Andrew fluffed the pillows behind her. "Better?"

"Mmm. Yes." She reached for his hand. "Are you ready to be a father again?"

He closed his eyes for a moment and his mouth turned down. "Yes, but, sweetheart, I'm scared. I don't want to lose you."

She squeezed his hand. "You won't lose me. I'm strong. This baby is strong and he's ready to be born."

"You always say he. Will you be disappointed if we have another girl?"

"Not in the least, but I believe this child is a boy. He's been kicking me for the last hour but now he's settled down and is getting ready to be born. Trust me, my love, all will be well."

Nora came in with the bucket of hot water and left it by the fireplace.

Four hours later, Doc finally walked into the bedroom. "I hear we're about to have a baby. Victoria, how long have you been having labor pains?"

"Since late last night. They kept me up all night."

Andrew turned to her, eyes wide. "Why didn't you tell me?"

"You couldn't do anything. They weren't close enough together to call Doc. They are now."

"How far apart are they now, Victoria?" asked Doc.

"Almost constant and all I want to do now is push. I'm ready to have this baby." Another contraction hit her and this time she couldn't stop the moan. The pain was worse and constant now.

"Let me get a look. Raise your knees and let's see what we have going on."

She raised her knees. Her nightgown slid to the top of her thighs.

Doc peered between her legs and chuckled.

"Looks like your little one is ready to be born. He's

crowning. Victoria, I want you to push, with the next contraction, as hard as you can."

She bore down with all her might, squeezing Andrew's hands as hard as she could, digging her nails into his palms. He was her anchor and she was glad he was there. Waves of pain circled her abdomen and all she wanted was for it to stop.

"Good girl," said Doc. "Now I want you to do that again. Push, bear down. Push, Victoria," demanded Doc.

She cried out and squeezed Andrew's hands, but bore down again and again and again until finally she felt the baby slide from her body.

"You have a boy," said Doc. He cleaned the baby's mouth out and the infant started to cry and take air into his lungs. "Okay, he's a fighter. Nora will you clean him up and give him to Mama and Daddy, please?" He handed the baby to Nora.

She took the baby over to the bureau where she'd set up the basin with wash cloths and towels. She also had the small blanket that Victoria had made.

Doc worked on Victoria to deliver the after birth. Then he placed thick cloths on her and covered her with the blanket on the bed.

"You did great Victoria. You were built to have children. You've got wide hips and shouldn't have any problems in the future, I don't believe. I'll take my leave now."

Victoria gave Andrew's hand a final squeeze. "See, my love. Doc said I'm made to have children."

"How much do I owe you, Doc?"

"Five dollars should do it."

Andrew dug in his pocket and came up with a five-dollar gold piece. "Here you go. Thanks, Doc."

"Any time. I'd much rather deliver babies than sew up gunshot wounds. You two enjoy your new son."

Doc left.

Nora had swaddled the baby and handed him to Victoria.

Victoria looked up. "Thank you, Nora. Thank you so much."

"You're welcome. This has been my favorite day since you came. I'll send in the rest of the family in about half an hour. Will that be all right?"

Andrew looked down at Victoria and his new son. "Make it fifteen minutes. In half an hour Victoria might be nursing."

"Fifteen minutes it is." Nora left the room, closing the door behind her.

Victoria quickly unwrapped the baby. He was long and thin. He didn't have much fat on him yet, but Victoria would see to that. She and Andrew counted his fingers and his toes.

Andrew put his finger in the baby's hand, and the infant closed his fingers around his father's finger.

Victoria thought she saw the moment Andrew fell in love with his son. The child looked like Victoria, with her brown hair. His eyes were blue but might turn to her gray ones. Luckily, he looked nothing like his sire. Victoria would never think of that incident again. He was her son, her and Andrew's son.

"What shall we name him? We chose Calvin, but I think I prefer Douglas. What do you think? He just doesn't look like a Calvin to me."

Andrew rubbed his thumb over the tiny fingers of his son. "Douglas Mayfield. For his middle name, how about Albert, after my father? Douglas Albert Mayfield. I like it. What about you?"

"Yup, Douglas it is and I like Albert, too."

She stroked her hand over the soft, downy brown hair and then brought the baby up for kisses. Victoria loved this child. Just looking at him made her heart full to near bursting.

Suddenly the door burst open and Suse came running in, followed more slowly by David and Margie.

"May we come in?" asked David.

"Of course. You're family," said Victoria. "Come in and meet Douglas Albert Mayfield."

"He's too little," said Suse. "I call him Dougie."

Andrew smiled and took the baby from Victoria and got on his knees so Suse and Margie could see him.

"He's so little," said Margie. She had her hands behind her and rocked side to side.

"Can I hold him?" asked Suse.

"Not when he's so little. Only when Victoria or I are there and say you can. Understand? He's not one of your baby dolls, and you can't pick him up ever. Victoria or I will pick him up and put him in your lap when you're sitting."

She nodded, very solemnly. "Only when you say so."

"Andrew, let the girls come up on the bed next to me and they can touch him."

He lifted the children onto the bed.

"Suse, you be on this side, and Margie, you on my other side."

The girls settled in on either side of Victoria.

She left the baby unwrapped so the girls could touch him.

"He's so tiny," said Suse, her voice filled with awe. "He grow fast so we play together?"

"He'll grow fast, but probably not as fast as you want, and faster than your father and I want."

Margie touched his cheek and then rubbed his belly. "Can he be my little brother, too?"

Victoria looked at David—the man who had helped her and given her the wherewithal to start fresh, the man who, by his generosity, had set her life on a new course and, in a way, had given her Andrew, the love of her life.

"Yes, Douglas can be your little brother, too."

"I'm calling him Dougie like Suse."

Andrew smiled. "I think that is just fine."

Dougie began to fuss.

David clapped his hands. "All right, girls. Time to go. Dougie needs to eat."

Victoria swaddled the baby to keep him warm.

Andrew and David lifted their children from the bed.

David hustled the girls out and shut the door behind him.

Victoria opened her nightgown and put the baby to her breast. She teased his lips with her nipple until he latched on.

"Oh. Oww."

Andrew kissed her forehead. "Are you all right? According to Elise, when she nursed Suse, it hurts the first few times the baby nurses."

"It definitely doesn't feel good, I can tell you that."

Andrew sat on the bed next to her. "You'll be fine. You're a good mama."

"And you're a good father. Look how well Suse is taking this change. She could be jealous. Instead she wants to know when they can play." She looked up at him. "Are you still scared? You heard what Doc said, I'm made to have babies."

"I'll always be afraid. I love you too much to lose you."

Holding the baby in her right arm, she cupped his jaw with her left hand. "I love you, too. You'll never lose me. I'm not going anywhere. Not when I've found my own bit of paradise."

EPILOGUE

December 10, 1875

Victoria curled next to Andrew, their legs entangled and her head on his chest after having made love. The sun hadn't yet started to rise so it was still dark outside

"Happy anniversary, my love!" Andrew lay on his back in bed, an arm around her and the other behind his head.

"Can you believe I came here five years ago?"

"Barely. The time has flown. It seems like yesterday when you were giving birth to Dougie, and now he's almost five."

Small cries emanated from the cradle at the end of the bed.

Victoria started to rise. "Sounds like someone is hungry."

Andrew tightened his hold on Victoria, then kissed her forehead. "I'll get her."

He retrieved their seven-week-old daughter, Mary, from the cradle and returned to the bed.

"There now, Daddy's got you, and you're fine," he crooned before handing her to her mother.

Victoria sat up, put the baby to her breast and covered herself with a blanket. "You should probably put on your pants. You know the children will want to come in shortly and see their baby sister."

"What makes you think they don't come to see their mother and father?"

She rolled her eyes and lifted a brow. "Suse has come up with a reason to come in and join us in bed just about every morning since Dougie was born."

"Why do you think we are always making love in the dark?"

She frowned. "It's not dark. You have the lamp lit."

"You know what I mean."

She moved Mary to the other breast and let her nurse. Then she chuckled. "Yes, dear, I know what you mean and you're right. You could always put a lock on the door."

"I don't want to do that. I want them to learn to knock first and wait until we answer."

At that moment a knock sounded on the bedroom door, followed immediately by the door flying open and two-year-old John ran into the room. Dougie and Suse remained in the hallway.

"No, John," shouted Suse.

"John stop right there." Victoria held up her arm in a motion to stop.

The child slid to a halt in his socks.

"What did you forget?"

He shoved his first two fingers into his mouth. "I s'pose wait for Mama say come in."

"That's right. Now, go back out, close the door and do what you're supposed to do. Go on."

Dougie and Suse had not entered the room and so waited for their little brother to return to them.

Suse pulled the door shut.

A knock sounded.

Victoria looked at Andrew and then nodded.

"Come in," he said.

His deep voice did things to her insides as it always did when they were close.

The door opened and John peeked around the edge.

Andrew waved him inside.

The door slammed against the wall as all three children ran into the room.

John started to jump on the bed, but Andrew waved his finger back and forth and the child stopped at the side of the bed and crawled up between his parents.

Suse was on the outside of her mother.

Dougie was on the other side of his father.

They filled the bed to overflowing as it was every morning for a few minutes.

All too soon it was time to get up and get the morning chores started.

The scent of fresh coffee reached Victoria's nostrils, and she breathed in deeply.

Nora was already starting breakfast.

Suse, nearly eight, normally watched Mary while Victoria milked the cow and gathered the eggs. This time next year, both of those would be Suse's jobs, but today was a good day to start one.

"Okay, children, go get dressed. Suse, you get to gather the eggs this morning. You know how, so that will be your job from now on," said Victoria.

"Yes, Mama." Suse crawled off the bed and ran to her room.

"Go on boys," said Andrew. "You heard your mother. Get dressed. Dougie, you help John."

"Yes, Daddy," said Dougie.

"Yes, Daddy," echoed John.

As the boys left, Victoria called out. "Dougie, shut the door behind you."

He didn't respond but did as she asked.

She put Mary on her shoulder.

Andrew got her two diapers, one for her shoulder and one for the baby.

Victoria burped the baby and then changed her before giving Andrew his clean, little daughter.

"I never get over how small they are in my hands."

"That's because you have big hands and feet and—"

He grinned. "That's enough about my attributes."

She chuckled. Then she leaned over and, watching for the baby, kissed him long and completely.

"What was that for? Not that I minded, just so you know."

She smiled and ran a finger along his jaw. "Just that I love you, and I thank you for keeping me."

"I couldn't have sent you away. I already loved you, though I wouldn't admit it. And I love you more today than yesterday."

"I do you, too. I think I loved you the moment you didn't make love to me on our wedding night. And then there was the way you were with Suse. You clearly loved her. When you could have been gruff with her, you were gentle."

"After Elise died, Suse was my whole heart. At least the part that still felt anything. Then you came and my heart filled completely with love for you. Now." He looked down at the baby in his arms. "All of them and you fill my heart to bursting."

Her heart hurt at the thought of losing her family. "I feel the same way. I can't imagine my life without you and the children. I don't want to. If I lost you—"

He laid two fingers across her lips. "Shh. We won't speak of such things that won't happen. I would tell you tonight, but now is as good a time as any. I'm pulling back on my duties. I won't be working with the horses anymore. The younger men can green break them for the army and I won't be going on the cattle drives. Ray will handle that as part of his foreman duties, along with a pay raise."

"Oh, Andrew. I'm so happy. You have no idea how my heart drops if one of the men comes to the kitchen while you're with the horses. I tried to watch once and saw you bucked off. I was sure you broke your neck, but you stood, laughed and got back on. I knew then I couldn't watch anymore."

He tilted his head slightly and frowned. "I never saw you."

She shook her head. "You wouldn't have. I stood in the barn's shadow where I couldn't be seen and shoved my fist in my mouth when you fell."

He raised his knees and shifted Mary to lie on his thighs. Then he put an arm around her mother. "I'm sorry. I never knew. If I had, I would have done my best to ease your fears."

She furrowed her eyebrows. "What could you have said? *Believe me, I won't be hurt?* Like I would believe that after what I saw. At least then I knew where you got your bruises."

"Ah, honey, I'm so sorry. I love you so much, and I hate that I made you worry so."

She cuddled in next to him. "It's all right now. You've made me the happiest woman in the valley."

"Good. Because I know I'm the happiest man."

"I love you."

"And I you."

For the first time, Mary giggled.

ABOUT THE AUTHOR

Cynthia Woolf is an award-winning and best-selling author of forty-five historical western romance novels and six sci-fi romance novels, which she calls westerns in space. Along with these books she has also published four boxed sets of her books.

Cynthia loves writing and reading romance. Her first western romance Tame A Wild Heart was inspired by the story her mother told her of meeting Cynthia's father on a ranch in Creede, Colorado. Although Tame A Wild Heart takes place in Creede that is the only similarity between the stories. Her father was a cowboy not a bounty hunter and her mother was a nursemaid (called a nanny now) not the owner of the ranch.

Cynthia credits her wonderfully supportive husband Jim and her great critique partners for saving her sanity and allowing her to explore her creativity.

STAY CONNECTED!

Newsletter

Sign up for my newsletter and get a free book.

Follow Cindy

https://www.facebook.com/cindy.woolf.5
https://twitter.com/CynthiaWoolf
http://cynthiawoolf.com

ALSO BY CYNTHIA WOOLF

Bachelors and Babies

Carter

————

Brides of Homestead Canyon/Montana Sky Series

Thorpe's Mail-Order Bride

Kissed by a Stranger

A Family for Christmas

————

Bride of Nevada

Genevieve

————

Brides of the Oregon Trail

Hannah

Lydia

Bella

Eliza

Rebecca

Charlotte

————

Brides of San Francisco

Nellie

Annie

Cora

Sophia

Amelia

————

Brides of Seattle

Mail Order Mystery

Mail Order Mayhem

Mail Order Mix-Up

Mail Order Moonlight

Mail Order Melody

————

Brides of Tombstone

Mail Order Outlaw

Mail Order Doctor

Mail Order Baron

————

Central City Brides

The Dancing Bride

The Sapphire Bride

The Irish Bride

The Pretender Bride

————

Destiny in Deadwood

Jake

Liam

Zach

———

Hope's Crossing

The Stolen Bride

The Hunter Bride

The Replacement Bride

The Unexpected Bride

———

Matchmaker & Co Series

Capital Bride

Heiress Bride

Fiery Bride

Colorado Bride

———

The Surprise Brides

Gideon

———

Tame

Tame a Wild Heart

Tame a Wild Wind

Tame a Wild Bride

Tame A Honeymoon Heart

Tame Boxset

————

Centauri Series (SciFi Romance)

Centauri Dawn

Centauri Twilight

Centauri Midnight

————

Singles

Sweetwater Springs Christmas

Made in the USA
Las Vegas, NV
28 January 2021